SOMEONE'S GONNA GET IT

MYCHEA

Good2Go Publishing

Someone's Gonna Get It
Written by Mychea
Cover Design: Davida Baldwin
Typesetter: Mychea, Inc
ISBN: 9781943686469
Copyright ©2017 Good2Go Publishing
Published 2017 by Good2Go Publishing
7311 W. Glass Lane • Laveen, AZ 85339
www.good2gopublishing.com
https://twitter.com/good2gobooks
G2G@good2gopublishing.com
www.facebook.com/good2gopublishing
www.instagram.com/good2gopublishing

Acknowledgments

To my faithful readers.
This one's for you.

SOMEONE'S GONNA GET IT

ONE

"DADDY!" A YOUNG, WIDE-EYED CHILD OF FIVE SCREECHED AS *she appeared to fly rather than run through the open front door up to the tall, handsome man walking up the pink and yellow tulip-lined sidewalk toward the house, elated that her father had returned home.*

"Princ—" His words cut short as a whizzing sound caressed his ear and a hollow-point bullet lodged itself in the back of his head, forcing his towering body to free fall through the air, immediately hitting the ground with a hard thud. Kara watched tragically as a fray of bullets followed and specs of blood rained over her petite body in her virginal white sundress. She let out a blood-curdling scream, filling the once peaceful, lazy afternoon with alarm. The love of her life lay facedown before her.

"What is happening?" a frantic feminine voice shouted from the inside the house. "Kara, honey, get down!"

Kara was oblivious to the command as she watched the red liquid gush out of the place her father's head once occupied.

"Oh, my God! Kara, duck, honey, duck!" The woman ran hastily from the house, trying her best to dodge bullets as she leapt onto Kara, using her body as a shield, forcing the little girl to the ground.

Continuing to inhale small breaths as she tried to regulate her breathing, Kara slowly stood on wobbly legs.

Making her way sluggishly to the other end of the room, she made a quick pit stop to grab her 9mm Glock out of her nightstand on the way. Peering through her sheer black silk curtains at the darkness caused by the cloudy sky, she missed the shine of the moonlight. Pushing the curtains to the side, she gazed down at the peaceful street, where nothing seemed out of place, and wondered if she was really losing her mind lately.

Silly girl. No one is watching you. Breathing easier now after confirmation of no one glaring up at her through the darkness, Kara managed a small apprehensive smile. *I have to get it together.* Approaching the anniversary of her father's death was messing with her psyche, and as a detective in the line of duty, she couldn't afford to have these types of distractions.

Returning the loaded weapon to the nightstand, Kara retrieved her cell phone, trying to fight back the urge to call Jason. Her fingers seemed to have a mind of their own as they dialed the first three digits of his 703 Northern Virginia number.

Rational logic pushing emotion to the side, she deleted those three digits, choosing to dial her mother instead. Kara refused to let Jason have the satisfaction of her being the first one to call after he had ended their engagement no less than a month ago. Jason with his boyish good looks and Colgate smile. Graduating from Harvard University with an MBA, you would think he was the snobbish type, but not by a long shot, when she had first met him. Now was a different story however. She recalled their first meeting taking place by happenstance.

"Misty, I cannot run another minute," I told her in anguish as I bent down at the waist to suck in air and give my tortured limbs a break. This was no way to spend the day before my twenty-first birthday, three days before Thanksgiving. I know I was the one that had tasked her to train with me, but we'd been running for over an hour. My legs were feeling like cooked spaghetti; I just knew that any second I was going to fall flat on my face in the middle of the street.

"I'm not buying that. You want to be a quitter, or you want to be the best?" she shouted, jogging in place.

"Right now, I'd settle for quitter," I mumbled. The shrill sound of the whistle being blown beside my ear made me wince.

"What was that, cadet? No quitters on my watch. Let's get moving," Misty shouted as she began jogging down the street leaving me to drown in my self-pity alone.

I cringed. Best friend or not, she was sitting on the one good nerve that I had left, and I didn't particularly care for her at the moment. Chest heaving up and down, breathing irregularly, lungs debating on whether to shut down and put us both out of our misery, I knew I was at the point of passing out, but I refused to let her get the best of me. So, engrossed as I was in my own head, I neglected to hear the persistent beeping of the car horn behind me.

"Kara, look out!" Misty yelled from her stance down the street as I glanced to see her running back in my

3

direction waving her hands frantically back and forth; but it was too late. Much too late. I could hear brakes squealing as the driver of the Mercedes pressed down on them firmly, in the vain hopes of avoiding the foolish woman intent on standing in the middle of the street. The dark unknown welcomed me.

I regained consciousness suddenly in a hospital bed, with the sweet smell of lemon drifting up my nostrils. My body felt as if I'd been run over by a car; exactly as it should. I cringed.

"You're awake," a deep masculine voice spoke to me, standing just outside of my peripheral. With my head throbbing the way it was, there was no way I could turn in his direction.

Speech left me as this magnificent creature entered my line of vision, his face etched in concern.

"Are you alright?" Running his hands through his hair, he bowed his head sheepishly. "Of course you're not alright. Look what I did to you."

"You did?" I questioned, my raspy voice sounding foreign to even my own ears. "I thought I put me here, being the idiot running in the middle of the street. I should have expected a car to hit me."

"I should have seen you. My phone rang, I looked down for one second, and when I looked back up, there you were—an apparition in the suburbs." His brown eyes speckled with gold and green were sad. "I truly am sorry. I've been sitting here waiting for you to wake up to express my sincerest apologies."

"You've been here the whole time? How long have I been here?"

"About forty-eight hours."

"Really?" I was shocked to find that I had been out of it for two days. "Where is Misty, the woman that was with me?"

"She had to leave, but your mother is here. She went down to the cafeteria to eat, thinking she had enough time before you woke up. It's the first time she's left your side since she arrived."

"My mom." Tears sprang to my eyes. I'm so glad I survived this. My mom couldn't go through another tragedy in her lifetime. It would just be too much for one person to handle.

"Hey, no tears. You survived, and I for one am grateful," the magnificent creature said.

My lips turned up slightly at the ends. "Sounds like you are just hoping to avoid a massive lawsuit."

"I never avoid anything."

I immediately regretted my statement. He seemed genuinely offended.

"Whatever you need I will pay. My main concern is that you are alright."

I believed him. He had that wholesome good-guy thing going on. You could tell that his parents had raised him right.

"I think I'll be okay. My body feels like I've been run over, but other than that, I'll live."

"My" creature gave a full-on commercial-worthy smile.

5

Had a Cologate representative been standing in my hospital room with us, he would have gotten a contract right there on the spot. Under more appropriate circumstances, minus the bandages and sterile room, I may have flirted with him.

"Technically you have been run over a little." His smile faded. "I truly am sorry."

"You said that already."

My creature took my hand into his. "I want you to know that I mean it."

Gazing into those mesmerizing eyes, I almost said, "If this is what happens when you get hit by a car, please feel free to hit me anytime."

"I know that you mean it. Thank you for staying with me."

"I'm Jason McCarthy by the way, and the pleasure has been all mine."

"Kara, are you alright?" her mother's sleepy voice came across the phone line.

"Yes, Mom, I'm sorry to wake you. I couldn't sleep."

"Oh no, my poor cupcake, another one of your nightmares?"

"Yes ma'am." She omitted her suspicion about feeling as if she were being watched. Kara didn't want her mom worrying more about her than she needed to.

"I knew with the anniversary of your dad's passing looming near that this would be a hard time for you."

"Mom, I don't want to talk about Daddy." A rainfall of

tears threatened to race down her face.

"Oh, but, darling, you really need to talk about him to someone."

"I have a standing appointment with my therapist every other Tuesday. She and I will touch base at our next session."

"Okay, honey. Will you be alright for the rest of the night? You can drive over here if you feel up to it," her mother offered.

"No, I'll be okay. Thanks for the offer. Go on back to sleep."

"Okay. Call me back if you need to. Good night. I love you."

"I will, Mom. I love you more. Night."

TWO

TIME IS TICKING; TICKING DOWN. NOSE PRESSED TO THE spotless windowpane, I watch her slumber. Night after night this has become a favorite pastime of mine as her soft dark brown hair cascades down the pillowcase in waves. Every night she tosses and turns attempting to find comfort in her dreams, a comfort that escapes her night after night.

Climbing through the unlatched window I had unlocked earlier that afternoon, I walk to her bed undetected as she lies lost in a sea of unconsciousness—our bedtime ritual, if you will. I've put her to bed every night since her father was murdered. My due diligence for the deeds I've done. I was her parent of sorts; she wouldn't see it that way, but that's who I am. I will be there until that moment when she takes her last breath, and then I can smile in victory.

THREE

"I STILL CAN'T BELIEVE WHAT JASON DID. HE CAN BE SUCH AN asshole. He had me completely fooled. He never came off to me as that type of guy. The bad-boy guy. So out of character for him."

"You know what, Misty? You learn new things about people every day. No one is ever quite how they appear to be at first. We all thought he was a good guy. What a joke. He fooled all of us."

"Can you kill the Debbie Downer syndrome today? People aren't that bad."

"If you say so." Kara was unsure of why Misty seemed instantly irked by her statement. She watched through the windows as the captain stopped outside her office door. "Misty, I'm a call you back," she whispered, quickly returning the phone to its cradle.

Not that she couldn't be on her desk phone, but as one of two female detectives in her unit, she felt as if she had to set a precedent and hold herself accountable to a higher standard. One of them was to not be chatting on the phone like a school girl to your best friend about your ex-fiancé. It was hard enough to gain respect as a woman on the force. No need to give them any free ammunition for a gunfight she knew was inevitable to come, that she would be unable to stop.

"Captain," Kara acknowledged him as she stood up.

"Anthony." He nodded at her with his faithful toothpick in his mouth dangling from his lip defying gravity as only he could seem to do. Kara eyed him warily, hating the fact that he called her by her last name as he shuffled into her office taking a seat in her chair, placing what looked to be size eleven feet on her desk and crossing his ankles.

She was disgusted. She knew in her heart that if she were a man, this blatant display of disrespect would not be happening.

"Sir."

"I have a new case I'd like you to work on."

Kara remained silent. The captain was one of those men that liked to feel as if he was more important than he was. There was no reason for him to be down here in her office delivering a case to her personally. A phone call would have sufficed.

"It's back in your neck of the woods."

"What's my neck of the woods?"

"Over in Southeast."

"Why are you sending me there?" Kara worked in the Fifth District of the police department. She had worked hard to leave the Seventh District, where her Captain was trying to send her back to. She didn't like working that area. She'd grown up there, and after having run-ins with many of her old neighborhood buddies who got into trouble with the law, she had requested to be transferred out of that district.

"The Spellman case you worked on a few years ago."

Kara's heart filled with dread. The Spellman case was a case she tried her best not to think about and up until now had avoided at all costs.

"I vaguely recall the case." She told a little white lie.

Her captain gave her a knowing glance. "I know this will be difficult for you, but Ryan is up for parole and they need you there at his parole hearing."

"I'm unclear as to why I am needed." She pressed the issue. Her testimony had placed Ryan Spellman behind bars five years ago, when she'd first entered the force as a police officer. "If he's up for parole that's fine. He should be allowed to go free. I won't stand in his way."

"You don't want to go and contest the parole?" her captain probed.

"No. Why would I do that? He's paid his debt to society. Let him try to regain access to his life." *It's only fair after what I did to him.*

"Nonsense," came her captain's gruff response. "There has been a new break in the case. I want you to go down there and figure out what's going on."

"Captain, with all due respect," Kara chose her words carefully, "I would prefer to step back from this case and let someone else have a hand at it. *It's personal*," she emphasized to give him an inkling of why she shouldn't be on the case.

"It's your old case. You will go down there and sort through the new evidence. End of discussion." His body language indicated that the conversation had concluded and Kara would be heading back down to District Seven to work on this case.

"Yes sir," she replied as he stood looking her square in the eye.

"Anthony, I know you can do this. You would never let a personal matter compromise your position on this force. Correct?" His gray eyes pierced through hers.

"You are correct," Kara conceded. She would not be the weak link. She could get through this.

"Great. I knew I could count on you. When Whitlock returns from vacation he can help you."

"Of course, you can count on me," she said, only mildly believing her own words. She couldn't wait for Kyle's return.

Kara dialed Misty's extension as soon as the captain breezed out of her office. "Come to my office right now." Urgency riddled her voice, and Misty made record time joining Kara in her office.

"What's going on?" she whispered, closing the door behind her.

"Captain Harris was just here."

"I know. I heard through the grapevine that he's trying to put you back on the Spellman case."

"Well he succeeded. I am back on the case. He didn't give me much of a choice. How am I the last one to know these things?"

"You know no one can keep a secret around these parts. What are you going to do?"

Kara gazed into Misty's concerned eyes. "I guess I'm headed on a road trip. I'm going to see Ryan." Kara sighed.

"Will you be okay?" Misty's face frowned up in concern.

"I'm going to have to be." Kara sighed. It had been so

long since she and Ryan had crossed paths, she knew this was sure to be an interesting experience. "I'm about to head down to District Seven to check out this new evidence. Ryan's parole is approaching. It seems mighty convenient that they find something at this precise time when he's already been locked up for the past five years."

"It does seem a little suspicious." Misty nodded in agreement.

"It's a lot suspicious." Kara was grateful that Misty was there. As the only two females in the department, they relied heavily on one another. "I'm headed out. I will keep you posted."

"Please do."

Stepping into FCI Butner Medium II Federal Correctional Institution in North Carolina where Ryan was housed, Kara made her way through their security points, checking her weapon at the front. She was feeling anxious as she waited in the holding room for Ryan to come down. Kara knew without a doubt that he wouldn't be thrilled to see her, but here she was anyway, ready to do what was right. It was long overdue, and time for Ryan to be free.

"Why are you here?" They were the first words Ryan had spoken to Kara in over five years. Kara took in his appearance. Gone were the warm, friendly almond-brown eyes that used to smile at her in admiration. Barely contained hate was replaced in them now. She could feel the rage radiating from him. Ryan, the first love of her life, the guy with plans to play pro football. Now his lean body seemed better suited for a swimmer.

"I'm glad you agreed to see me. I miss you. It's been a long time," she began softly, timidly.

"Apparently not long enough." He sat erect in his chair, hostile.

"I deserve that." Kara took in his appearance. Gone was the jovial guy she once knew. This person before her in his wrinkled orange jumpsuit and dirty sneakers was a stranger to her. "But, Ryan, despite what you think, I'm here to help."

"How can you possibly help with anything?" His voice rose in anguish. "*You're* the reason I'm here. Why would you want to help me now? And what makes you think I would take your help? I know a setup when I see one, and I could smell you from a mile away."

I did this to him. Don't react negatively. He's just angry with you, as he has every right to be. Kara had to keep reminding herself. She was the reason Ryan was here, and looking at him now she realized his sacrifice was too much for her to bear. She should be the one behind bars, not him. How had she allowed this man to take a fall for her and just left him here? What kind of person was she to do this to her friend, a friend she had loved dearly?

"Because I want to right this wrong. Please let me do that." Ryan stared at Kara a long time without blinking, so long that Kara began to squirm under his intense gaze, feeling exposed as the fraud that he probably believed she was. It made her uncomfortable, because maybe she was a fraud, and that was a hard pill to swallow.

Eventually letting out a low sigh, Ryan relaxed his body. Kara was ecstatic about this one small victory.

"You know you have to marry me now, right?" Ryan's dimpled smile was infectious. Kara grinned in return.

"Oh yeah, why is that?"

"Because I love you and I have to be with you forever."

"Is that right?"

"That's right." He took her left hand into his, sliding a small diamond ring onto it. "It's not much now, but once I make it to the NFL I'll buy you a bigger one."

Kara smiled. "You won't dare." She beamed at the petite heart-shaped ring. "This one is perfect. I love it and I love you."

Ryan leaned down, his tall six-foot-two frame practically toppling over her petite frame of five four.

"Alright. I'll listen to what you have to say."

Kara shook the memory off when Ryan spoke.

"Thank you for agreeing to meet with me. I want to begin by apologizing to you about this entire situation. All of this is wrong. Very, very wrong, and I am so sorry."

"Can you stop apologizing? I don't believe it anyway." Ryan was not the least bit impressed with her "I'm sorrys." He was angry, but not so angry that he wasn't curious as to why she had come calling on him after no contact for the last five years.

Kara kept seeing "fraud" flashing in her mind.

"Do you ever wonder what our life would have been like if that awful night had never happened?" She offered a soft smile in his direction. "We'd be married, maybe with kids by now. What a difference life would be, right?"

"Glad I dodged that bullet. Besides, I'm married." Ryan wasn't in the mood for Kara's what-if games or thinking about a time that could have been theirs and never was. Their time was done. He had moved on and could only focus on the now. The innocent kid he was back then no longer existed. Kara could blame herself for that.

The woman that dated Ryan and was his fiancée in another time and place wanted to cry her eyes out, but that's not what she had come here for. The older, wiser woman in her today was glad that he'd found happiness. Even if it was behind these institutionalized walls; even if it wasn't her. Even if she should have chosen the life with Ryan, especially after what Jason had dealt her. Ryan would never have left her. *So why did I feel that it was okay to leave him?*

"I'm glad to hear it. I'm happy for you, Ryan." She grabbed his hand. "Truly I am."

Ryan stared into her eyes and allowed himself to squeeze her hand, giving in to remembering what they once were to each other; but understanding where they were now and that they couldn't go back to a time that no longer existed, he let her hand go.

"Okay, tell me why you're here," he said abruptly, allowing Kara her time to elaborate on her presence after five years of radio silence.

FOUR

"THIS IS JUST PERFECT," KARA GROANED UNDER HER BREATH, ignoring Misty's call on her cell and placing the phone on the hall table as she opened the door wide letting Jason inside her Northeast DC rented townhome. "To what do I owe the pleasure, Mr. McCarthy?" She'd been home for a few hours from her road trip to see Ryan, only to have Jason pop up on her doorstep.

"We need to talk." He pushed past her into the foyer.

Talk? Kara was bemused. *Now he wants to talk.* "Why would you want to talk to me?" Closing the door behind him she folded her arms across her chest. "I distinctly remember your last words to me being, 'It's not working. We have *nothing* left to say to one another and should go our separate ways.'" Kara pointed to his chest. "That was you who said that, right? Please correct me if I'm wrong or missing anything."

Jason sheepishly flashed that stupid Colgate smile she had come to loathe—a smile that was easily worth a million-dollar ad on a billboard in Times Square—and Kara resisted the urge to punch him square in the face, maybe take a few teeth out with her punch. The thought of a snaggletooth Jason made her smile, and her heart lightened a little.

"I see you're in the usual Kara mood today." His deep voice penetrated her thoughts, irritating her all over again, lightened heart forgotten.

Kara closed her eyes and willed herself not to be baited

by him. Her therapist would be proud of her. *Kara one, Jason zero.*

"Jason, what can I do for you?" she questioned, doing her best to take the edge out of her voice. The sooner she cooperated with him, the sooner he would be returning to from where he had come.

"I brought this for you." He handed a folded newspaper out to her.

Kara reached for the *The Washington Post* he handed her, brow arched, trying to understand why Jason had decided to take up a new profession as her paperboy.

"Why? Surely there is not an outage of paper delivery boys. Life minus Kara must equal hard times." She couldn't resist the jab. She was working on being better; she never said that she was perfect, however, and Jason in all his handsome, perfect splendor made her want to wipe all that cool confidence off his face.

"You would like that, wouldn't you?" Jason retorted, leaving her standing by the front door as he entered the family room off to the left of the narrow hallway. "Sorry to disappoint, but I'm doing extremely well. No hard times over here, ever. Though if you need some help, I'm sure I can help you out."

"Thanks, but no thanks. I wouldn't take your help if I was on fire and you were the last one standing with a bucket of water," Kara spat as trying to keep her cool was going by the wayside as she followed in his wake. Entering the room, she saw him frowning as he picked up and returned a framed photo of the two of them smiling into each other's eyes at a gala last year, back on her glass coffee table. She could have kicked herself for not removing the photos of the two of them by now. She just couldn't bring herself to do it. Everything seemed more final when you took photos down. She hadn't been ready to see her table devoid of their memories just yet.

"If you're here to torture me, you can leave. I didn't invite you here," she reminded him, wondering for the fifth time since she opened the door why Jason was once again in her house.

Jason cleared his throat in a rare display of discomfort. "Look at the paper."

She glanced down. She'd forgotten about the paper in her hands. Unfolding the *Post* to the front page of the society section, she felt her heart drop as she came face-to-face with a full-page article and half-page photo of Jason and Misty dancing in each other's arms as the new Mr. and Mrs. Jason McCarthy.

God must have been friends with Jason, because Kara had locked her gun upstairs in the safe tucked away in the closet. *If it hadn't been for that small casualty, Jason would be shot, bleeding out on my hardwood floor, living out his last moments begging me for mercy and forgiveness.*

"What is this?" Kara yelled, throwing the paper at his head. *So much for keeping my cool.*

"Are you crazy?" He ducked as the paper came within an inch of his scalp and hit the wall.

Before he could fully recover from ducking, Kara lunged at him, with tears cascading down her face. "How could you do something like this?" she asked, her years of boxing to reduce stress displaying how skilled she was with her fists.

Jason did his best to ward off her punches as he dodged around the room. If the situation hadn't been so dire, Kara might have laughed at how ridiculous the two of them must have looked.

"You came over here to tell me *this*?"

Jason tackled her, and they both hit the floor with a loud thud. Kara winced as her body hit the wood under his weight, knowing that a bruise would be forming on her backside.

"Stop acting like a child and listen."

"There is nothing to listen to. Any explanation you have you can keep. Whatever you have to say isn't good enough as far as I'm concerned. You and Misty. I can't believe this."

"I wanted you to hear it from me before anyone had a chance to tell you. It's a lot to take in, and I don't want you to be embarrassed. You did nothing wrong."

"Gee, thanks for your concern, since you are the one embarrassing me. You can just shove it, okay. How could you two do this?" Kara shook her head in anger and disbelief. "This is not right. I don't deserve this. I have always loved you both. How could you? You two were my family."

"It wasn't planned, Kara. You have to believe me. It's something that just happened. It was bigger than both of us and we couldn't resist."

Kara scooted back on the floor once Jason lifted his body off hers, attempting to place much-needed space between her and him before her anger got the best of her and she socked him again. "There is no such thing as something like this just happening." *He married Misty. I cannot believe this. My ex-fiancé, my best friend. My best friend, my ex-fiancé. This is a cruel, cruel joke, and it's not funny. I must be being punked right now. Where is Ashton Kutcher and the camera crew? This is not funny, and it cannot be real. It just can't be. I won't accept this.*

"Kara, listen to me. It really is not as bad as you think it is." Jason ran his fingers through his wavy brown hair. Kara had never hated him more, with his Josh Harnett good looks and his Brad Pitt leaving for another woman ways. She could kill him at this moment, and if it hadn't been for her daily routine of locking up her weapon, he would have been dead by now. She began to wonder if he had become religious recently and that's why his life had been spared. She would have been able to get off for a crime of passion. She was sure of it.

"Please leave." Once again, her therapist would have gleamed with pride; now that she had a handle on her emotions a little, she was able to behave in a more rational, controlled manner.

"Not before I explain." Jason reached for her.

"If you touch me, I will gut punch you so hard you won't be able to keep your food down for a month. So help me God. Maybe you have forgotten that I am licensed to carry a weapon. I have no problem going to get it," Kara reminded him. "Please leave," she repeated more forcefully this time, rising to her feet.

Jason stood to his feet as well. "Suit yourself. I was attempting to let you know so you were prepared when people asked you about it. I was doing a favor. Misty warned me that it would be a bad idea."

Kara lunged at Jason again, knocking him to the ground for the second time. So much for rational behavior, hearing him utter Misty's name was too much for her sanity. This time she gave him a shiner in his right eye, smiling in satisfaction as his eye began to immediately puff up. She didn't lift weights and train with the guys at the station for nothing. Moments like these she appreciated the grueling physical demands of her profession.

"Fuck!" he exclaimed. She could tell by his tone and the cursing that he was furious. Jason with his fanciful pedigree and multiple degrees thought that expletives were beneath him and if one truly had an extensive vocabulary that they would never use such words to express themselves. This known fact brought Kara more joy as she smiled. Finally, she felt vindicated: Jason McCarthy had lost his cool. The world was spinning back in her favor.

"Fine. I'm leaving." He stood to his feet, walking toward the front door.

"Thank you. That is all I wanted you to do. We could have avoided this whole situation," she pointed out to him. "Next time you get the bright idea to come by unannounced, don't," Kara told him as she followed behind him and locked the door after his exit.

Her cell vibrating on the hall table caught her attention. Twenty missed calls, all from Misty with twenty accompanying voicemails. *She has some nerve.* Speaking of the devil himself, the phone began vibrating in her hand as Misty's name came across the screen again.

"Hello."

"Since when is punching people in the face okay?" Misty's haughty, demanding tone came across the line. "Who do you think you are, Kara? You don't have the right to walk around attacking people."

Kara removed the phone from her ear in stunned silence, staring at it for a prolonged minute. Misty had called to chastise her? Now she knew for a fact that there was a God in heaven, because Jason and Misty had a one-way ticket straight to hell. She raised the phone back to her ear only to hear Misty was still in the middle of ranting.

"I can't believe you," Kara said into the line, cutting her off. "You and Jason must be drinking the same type of delusional tea. You're both crazy."

"Don't tell me that you are over there trying to justify your actions."

"My actions are justifiable. You and Jason deserve each other. Please don't call me again. As a law officer, I would hate to have to get a restraining order on you for harassment. That would really hurt your chances of a promotion in our unit, now wouldn't it?"

"You wouldn't dare," Misty's undignified tone came across the line.

"Try me and see. You and Jason can burn in hell for all

I care." Kara hung up the phone, immediately dialing Dr. Jones.

"Kara, what a pleasant surprise," her therapist's jovial voice came across the line. "How are you?"

"Not good. I need to see you as soon as possible. Do you have an opening today?"

"Let me see here." Kara could hear the pages flipping in the calendar book that Dr. Jones famously carried everywhere she went. "I do have an opening at six today."

"I'll take it." Kara was desperate. If she didn't see Dr. Jones today she knew she would lose the little bit of sanity she was holding on to. Staring at the framed photo on her coffee room table of her and Jason smiling into each other's eyes, she quickly picked up the photo frame and threw it at the wall with all her might. She smiled with glee as it hit the wall and shattered to the floor in a million pieces.

FIVE

"WHAT IN THE WORLD HAPPENED WHEN YOU WENT OVER there?" Misty demanded as a bruise-eyed Jason came stumbling through their front door.

"She completely lost her cool. I've never seen Kara act like that before."

"I didn't even know she had it in her to be attacking somebody. Let alone you."

"I knew I should have handled this a while ago. We never should have run that story in the society paper, but you just had to have your name and picture all over it, didn't you?"

"Now wait a minute." Misty was mildly offended. "Don't go getting all hostile with me because Kara turned into Bruce Lee on you."

"Not funny, Misty. I find nothing amusing about any of this."

Misty left Jason in the foyer so he could feel sorry for himself alone. He was not going to make her feel bad about wanting the world to know she was Mrs. Jason McCarthy. This had been her come-up, and she knew people would be jealous to their core when they saw the one-page article and photo. She'd had to call in a special favor to get it done on such short notice. She didn't want there to be anyone questioning what it was she and Jason had going, especially Kara.

"I think we made a mistake." Jason finally came to where Misty was.

"A mistake. What is that supposed to mean, Jason? I don't think there was any mistake, so please tell me what you are referencing."

"Me, you, this, us. I can't believe I did this to Kara. She was right in telling me she didn't deserve this. She doesn't. She never did anything wrong. She was always a good woman to me. I'm the one that should be sorry. You and I both. She was good to us."

"Okay, so wait a minute. Are you telling me that you want to leave me already? We've barely been married for five minutes and you are trying to call it quits?"

"A McCarthy never admits defeat, and we don't get divorces, we're not built that way."

"Well that is good to know."

"I guess so. I feel trapped. I acted too fast. Something that I normally would never do." Jason shook his head. "What kind of spell did you put on me? I wasn't thinking clearly."

"Jason, this whole woe is me spirit thing has got to stop. We're married; it's done. You're just going to have to deal with it," Misty scolded him.

"You weren't there. You didn't have to look at her face when she read the news. She never should have found out that way." Jason was having a classic case of buyer's remorse. He'd seen the new cow, believed that it was better than his old cow, and was now missing the old cow. "Why don't you be a good little wife and get me some ice for my eye, instead of badgering me right now," Jason told her.

He'd had a long day. The last thing he wanted to be

engaged in was a debate with Misty about their marriage, which he'd felt good about up until he'd seen the hurt in Kara's eyes. He never wanted to see that look ever again. She'd looked like a wounded doe. He knew everything that had happened in her life, and he knew he'd never be able to fix what he'd done.

"No. Since you believe our union to be a mistake, you can ice your own eye. Serves you right treating me this way only a few weeks after our wedding. We should be in the honeymoon phase, not bickering over nonsense."

"My life is not nonsense." Jason made his way to the kitchen to pull out the ice, wondering how it had slipped past him that Misty could be such a shrew. *Maybe I can get an annulment instead of a divorce. No, Misty put your wedding on the society page, remember?* Jason sighed in anguish as he placed his ice in a Ziploc bag. *I could say I was temporarily insane, but then that may hurt my business. For all intents and purposes I'm stuck with Misty for the long haul. Damn.*

Walking down the hall to his study, he entered, locking the door behind him. Picking up his office line, he dialed a number and waited as it rang. On the third ring he was about to hang up, when he heard a hello.

"You answered."

"I know. Even though you don't deserve me to. Why are you calling?"

Jason cleared his throat a few times. "Because I owe you an apology."

"You really don't. We said our goodbyes already. Very

violently in fact. By the way, how is that eye?"

"Kara?"

"You don't owe me anything. I'll survive this. Just let me be."

"I'm an idiot. I love you."

"Who are you in there loving? Are you on the phone?" Misty was yelling through the door.

"You sure have a funny way of showing it." Kara didn't know why Jason was wasting his time calling her to begin with. The proof was in the pudding. He didn't love anyone nearly as much as he loved Jason, himself. She was just glad that she had found out sooner than later. He and Misty deserved each other. Even though she'd be lying if she said it didn't hurt her, she would survive this, the same way she survived everything else in her life. This would not break her.

"Thank you for even picking up the phone to talk to me."

"I'm just—" she paused "—I just wanted to see what you had to say. Even though I know it doesn't make up for anything, in my mind I thought we were building something. I thought we had a solid foundation, and you took that and what we had and just threw it away like it was nothing."

"I know," Jason said. "I regret that more than any-thing."

"Are you sure? We spent four years together. You know all my hopes and dreams, my aspirations, how many kids we were going to have. Why would we talk about all of those future plans if it wasn't going to be anything, or go anywhere?"

"I always wanted it to be something. It was something. I just wasn't ready."

"So then why not say something, you know? That's what couples do; they talk about their fears and what's going on, the challenges that come up in a relationship. You don't go all in marrying the next girl walking by. In this case, Misty. I just don't get it."

"Kara, you were right. You don't deserve the way I treated you. You deserve so much more than me, and I know you'll find that." *Why did I leave her?*

Kara stared at the phone loath to hang up but knowing there would be no forever with Jason and it was the right thing to do. No happily ever after, more like an unhappily never ever.

"Jason, I have to go," Kara whispered, surprising herself that she was remaining as calm as she was to speak with him at all.

"I know you do, and I have to let you go."

"Yeah, you do."

"Jason, you open this door right now!" Misty's brash tone broke the spell of the call.

"You should respond to her. She's not going to go away."

"I know. You take care of yourself."

"That's all I know how to do. Oh, and Jason?"

"Yes."

"I need you to do something for me."

"Anything." Jason gave no hesitation.

"Please don't contact me anymore. I want to be done with this and you after today. Have a good night."

Jason hung up the phone slowly as Misty continued knocking and yelling through his locked study door.

What have I gotten myself into?

"JASON!" Misty kicked the door. "You come out right now or I will knock this door down. Do you hear me?"

"The whole neighborhood can hear you. You're loud enough," Jason told her when he finally stood to open the door.

Misty eyed him skeptically. "Who have you been in here talking to?"

"None of your business. This is my private study, and I was handling an important matter that does not concern you."

"Everything you do needs to include me at all times."

"Is this a marriage or prison?"

"I don't know. You tell me," Misty demanded as she crossed her arms over her chest.

"Good night, Misty. I'm going to sleep in one of the guest rooms tonight. I need to be alone."

"That's fine, but don't make a habit of it. I would like to get started on a family."

Jason shook his head in disbelief, amazed by the audacity of this woman. He had just mentioned divorce tonight and feeling stuck in his marriage, and she was talking about having children. *You sure stuck your foot in it this time, didn't you, Jason? I sure did*, he responded to his own question in his head. This was going to be a long life, but he was determined to make it a short night.

SIX

DAY BY DAY, TICK BY TICK, MY DAY IS COMING. EACH TIME THE sun rises and sets I'm closer to my prey. I can taste her blood. I'm ready, but I am patient. Her day is coming. Watching her enter the building to visit her therapist, I parallel park across from the building to keep an eye out for her. I am proud of what she has been able to do with her life considering I took a big chunk out of it. Despite those odds, she rose above that. In a way I felt parental, as if I had the right. It doesn't matter. Soon I will have her in my clutches, and then she'll be all mine, to do with as I please. Knowing that she usually spends an hour with her therapist, I allow myself a thirty-minute nap. Even if she leaves before I wake, I'll know where to find her.

SEVEN

"THE NIGHTMARES HAVE RETURNED."

"I knew something must have been bothering you from the urgency in your tone." Kara enjoyed Barbara. She had been seeing her since she was an out of control teenager giving her mother nothing but grief. At her wits end, her mother had finally told her that if she didn't start talking to someone about her issues, she was going to have to get out of her house. That had been all the encouragement Kara needed to start getting her act together. She had decided that homelessness didn't suit her at all. Once she'd met Dr. Barbara Jones she had instantly felt secure in their sessions. Dr. Jones had a calming spirit about herself that she seemed to transfer to her clients. Her kinetic energy was amazing.

"Tell me about them," Dr. Jones gently probed.

"I keep going back to that day." Kara stared off into space.

"Guess who's coming home today."

"Daddy!" an excited Kara exclaimed. Her mother smiled.

"Yes, Daddy."

Kara knew the exact day: Wednesday, May 21, 1997. Her mother had bought her a Cinderella calendar because she wanted to be the golden-haired Princess so bad; to count the days until her father's return.

"We're baking cookies for Daddy," Kara sang.

"Yes, we are," her mother confirmed as the kitchen

wall phone rang. "Keep stirring, my little cupcake."

"Okay, Mommy."

"Hi, darling. We miss you so much," her mother said into the receiver.

"Is that Daddy? Can I talk to him?"

Shaking her head, her mother held her pointer finger to her lips indicating for Kara to be quiet. "What time will you arrive? What do you mean you don't know? Why are you doing this, Charles? What about Kay? She's been waiting for you. Fine, go be with them then." Her mother hung up the phone with a resounding slam.

"You okay, Mommy?" A concerned Kara paused from stirring the chocolate chips into the cookie dough to look at her mother.

"Yes, cupcake. I'm fine. You keep stirring, okay?" came back her mother's choked-up reply.

"Was that Daddy saying he missed me?"

"It sure was." Her mother forced a smile. "My sugar is so smart and sweet."

"I sure am." Kara smiled as she licked the spoon.

"Tell me what happened."

"I have good and bad memories. The nightmares are the bad ones, but every once in a while I have good ones and I remember what my mom and I were doing before my dad arrived home."

"What were you doing?"

"We were baking cookies, and then my dad called, but my mother wouldn't let me speak to him. Which I found strange because she always let me speak to my dad. And then she started crying."

"Have you ever spoken to her about that moment?"

"I tried to in the past, but Mother is adamant about not talking about it. Whatever transpired on that call, she fully intends to take it to the grave with her."

"How do you feel about that?"

Kara sat still and thought for a moment about how best to answer the doctor's question. "I feel hurt that she won't talk to me about it, won't share with me what was on her mind that day. But in a way I also feel as if she has the right to hold on to her last conversation with him and not share it with anyone."

"But." Dr. Jones mildly suggested that there was more to my statement.

"But I'm angry that she took that last conversation with my dad away from me. I want to hear his voice so bad. She took that from me. Robbed us of our last conversation."

"You sound very resentful."

"I am resentful."

"How has that played into your relationship until now?"

"Not too much. I don't not talk to her or not see her because of it. We have a normal, functioning relationship."

"And what is normal to you?"

"What do you mean?" Kara was a little taken back; wasn't *normal*, normal?

Dr. Jones pushed her black Vera Wang glasses up her nose and eyed Kara intently. "I mean, everyone has their own definition of normal." Her round face was pleasant as she peered at Kara. "I would like to know what yours is."

"I don't really know. The most *normal* I've ever felt is with Jason."

"Interesting that you bring up Jason and normal. Why do you feel that way?"

"I don't know." Kara shrugged. Why did she feel as if she were more normal when Jason was around? Could it be that he made her feel more alive?

"Come on, Kara, don't take the easy way out. I'm not letting you off the hook here," Dr. Jones pushed at her. "You mentioned him making you feel normal for a reason, so let's hear it."

Shifting on the chaise in Dr. Jones office, Kara respected the fact that Dr. Jones always, no matter the situation, held her accountable.

"Because with him I had emotions. He made me feel as if we could conquer the world together. His approval and reassurance meant a lot to me. I want to feel that again."

"You're using past tense. Has something happened between you two?"

Kara sighed, not really wanting to go into details, but feeling the need to unload this burden onto someone that could understand what she was going through.

"Dr. Jones, we just have so much to talk about today. I don't know where to begin." She leaned her head back until she was staring blankly straight up at the ceiling, not seeing, but feeling.

"Why don't you just relax? How about we do a few breathing exercises; then we can delve deep into the situation with you and Jason. I know with the anniversary of your father's death looming that everything right now may be hard for you coping-wise."

After five minutes of breathing exercises, Dr. Jones had been right; Kara felt much better and much more relaxed.

"I don't think there's enough time for me to get into what has gone down with me and Jason."

"You're my last appointment of the day, so you are free to take as long as you like." Dr. Jones removed her glasses and unbuttoned her suit jacket to get more comfortable. "Well, let's hear it," Dr. Jones stated.

"I don't know if I'm ready to talk about that," Kara told her honestly.

"Okay, you tell me where you would like to begin."

"So much has happened since the last time you and I sat down with one another. My ex-fiancé, the first one, is about to get out of jail. He's up for parole for a crime he didn't commit and has gotten married since he's been locked up."

"You never told me about your first ex-fiancé. Elaborate."

"Ryan is his name. My and Ryan's story is so complicated and chaotic. I'm not ready to share that with anyone. Maybe we should discuss my situation with Jason first."

"Fair enough. Please continue when you're ready."

"I'm ready now." Kara didn't want to wait in case she lost her nerve. "Jason breaks up with me no less than a month ago and up and marries Misty, my best friend. Then he had the nerve to stop by my house unannounced to show me the society page of the *Washington Post*, where there was a full-page feature on him and Misty's wedding. They both act like I'm the problem. I had no idea they were even dating behind my back. What kind of people do this sort of thing?" Kara looked at Dr. Jones hoping to find answers. She only smiled and nodded encouraging Kara to continue.

"All it does is explain to me the reason for the quick breakup and not wanting to discuss it or to work things out. I trusted them." The tears started. "I thought all of us were family, and they were plotting behind my back this whole time."

"That is a lot to take in during such a short time. How have you been handling that?" Dr. Jones asked.

"I'm not handling it well at all. It's just so much happening, and you're right, being so close to my father's twentieth anniversary, I haven't had time to focus on that, you know? I just have so much other stuff going on. I also feel as if I'm being watched. I believe someone is stalking me."

"Have you told the police?" Barbara asked, genuinely alarmed.

"I am the police, so to speak. That's like telling myself."

Dr. Jones gave her an exasperated look.

"No, I haven't said anything to anyone at the station yet."

"Okay, before we jump from topic to topic, let's back up for a moment. Safety is key. You need to let someone know your suspicions about feeling watched. Intuition generally doesn't lie. At the very least, what does it hurt for someone to ask around to make sure you're safe?"

Kara nodded in agreement with her question.

"Next, let's talk about Jason and Misty. Let's focus on that situation. How are you feeling about the two of them?"

"I feel betrayed by the two people I trusted and loved the most. You know, ever since my dad died, I don't really let people get close to me. I feel like I can't trust anyone, so to let those two in and have the two of them do something of this magnitude, it really hurts me, cuts me to the core."

"Your reaction is warranted. Are you angry?"

"Yes, I'm very angry. I want to hit something and hit it hard. Destroying it. I want somebody to suffer for what I've been through. I want my father. I miss him." Kara broke down into a fresh onset of tears that wouldn't stop.

"Bingo." Dr. Jones handed her the tissue box off her desk. "That's the real issue. You miss your father. That's the root of all of this. You have to make peace with him and his murderer. I know it's much easier said than done, but, Kara, you have to let this go. Forgive everyone involved. Only then will you be set free and know genuine peace."

Forgive everyone involved? She didn't even know everyone involved. She wished that she did. She needed someone to project her anger onto and seek justice for her father. Maybe that would be the best gift she could give him. Find the person that had started this twisted cycle. She needed to find her father's murderer.

EIGHT

DRIVING HOME AFTER HER THERAPY SESSION, KARA WAS pleased that she felt better after unloading everything into Dr. Jones's listening ear. *She has a way of making me feel so much better about myself. I can conquer the world now.*

"Hi, Mr. Li." Kara waved to the older Asian man. She had been coming to the same cleaners, Tash Cleaners on Benning Road close to Wings and More Wings, next to the hair salon hidden on a little side street in Northeast, for five years, since she first moved into the neighborhood. She loved the atmosphere and the urban feel of the area. Plus, it was a two-minute drive from her townhouse on 17th Place.

"Hi there, Kay."

Kara smiled. "You ready for me?"

"Always ready for you." His grin was infectious. As he pulled her clothing items from the rack.

"Thank you so much. You're so good to me." She winked at him, taking her clothes and sliding the hundred-dollar bill into his hand, paying for a ten-dollar dry-cleaning bill. "Here's a little something extra for being my favorite."

He blushed.

"See you next week." Kara retreated back to her car whistling a happy tune in spite of the recent events that had taken place in her life. *This too shall pass*, she recited happily in her head. That was something her mother had always instilled in her growing up: this too shall pass. Today that simple statement was working miracles on her heart, her mind, and her body.

Glancing out of her rearview mirror as she sat at the stop sign patiently waiting for the car in front of her to turn, she noticed that the black SUV behind her had to be going at least 60 mph, showing no signs of slowing down. In a panic Kara was about to pull forward, but the car in front of her had stopped driving, blocking her escape. Bracing for the worst Kara closed her eyes and willed her body to relax. She knew accidents were worse on your body if you were tense and scared at the time of impact instead of relaxed. She quickly reached for the radio in her car. "I'm about to be in an accident at the corner of C Street and 17th Place. Hurry," she radioed in.

Please let me survive this. The truck behind her collided with her car, pushing her into the black SUV that had stopped in front of her, blocking her escape.

Waking up inside of a Washington Hospital Center bed for the second time in her life was frightening. She thanked the good Lord she was still on this earth to breathe the fresh air, but she would be lying if she said her body was not in pain.

"Oh good, you're awake." A friendly nurse wearing the name tag Mia walked in to check her vitals. "You gave us quite a scare there, missy. We thought we had lost you for a moment."

"Really?" Kara croaked. "How bad am I?"

"Well—" Mia picked up Kara's chart hanging on the bottom of the bed "—you have three fractured ribs, a broken toe, two broken fingers, and a broken collarbone. You also have a concussion and a broken nose."

"Not too shabby, huh?" Kara's smile pressed through her grimace.

"I love a sense of humor." Nurse Mia placed the chart back at the end of the bed. "Keep that up." Mia smiled at her, patting her good hand. "You have a visitor."

"Is it my mother?"

"You'll see, darling. I'll send them right in."

Kara closed her eyes, doing her best not to fall asleep.

"We've got to stop meeting like this."

Groaning at the sound of the voice, Kara wished the hospital bed could swallow her whole. *Why me, God?*

"Jason, what are you doing here?" Kara wasted no time on pleasantries.

"I came to check on one of my favorite girls."

Kara wished she was able to stand up and move around. She was at his mercy stuck on this hospital bed, and he knew that.

"I see your face healed nicely."

Jason's face turned a bright crimson red. Kara relished in the small victory. The more uncomfortable he felt, the sooner he would leave.

"I'll let that slide considering your circumstances and the fact that I'm sure your face looks ten times worse under those bandages."

Kara pressed the nurse's button.

"You rang, Ms. Anthony." Kara was grateful Nurse Mia had returned.

"I'm feeling a little spent. Unless it's my mother, I would like to hold all my visitors."

"Sure thing, Ms. Anthony." She glanced over at Jason. "Sir, I'm sorry, but you'll have to leave now."

Jason glared at Kara. "I can't believe you're having me thrown out by the nurse."

Eyes closed, Kara pretended not to hear him. *Please go away.* Her last thought before drifting back off to sleep.

Groggily coming to as the nurse took her blood pressure, Kara was able to make out a vase of white roses and a card on the table next to her bed.

"What's that?" she asked the nurse, who was not Mia, sleepiness present in her wary voice.

"Oh, those were dropped off for you while you were napping." The nurse beamed at her. "Aren't they lovely?"

"Yes, they are lovely. Can you pass me the card?"

"Sure." The nurse gently shifted Kara's bed up to an upright position. "Here you are, dear. If it's uncomfortable sitting at this angle let me know."

"Thank you."

"You're welcome, honey. Here you are." She handed Kara the envelope. "I'll be right outside. If you need me press the button."

"I'll be sure to do that. Thank you again."

Kara waited until the nice gray-haired nurse exited the room, before flipping the flap open on the envelope. An inexplicable chill tap danced down her spine.

MYCHEA

You fought to see another day.
You're much stronger than I thought.
The clock is ticking, my dear . . . don't you hear it
in the distance?
Tick tock, goes the clock, tick tock, the heart stops.
Count darling, count.
Tick Tock.

NINE

GOING THROUGH THE BOXES OF FILES SHE'D HAD DELIVERED to her home, Kara was happy to be out of the hospital. After a month's time, her healing process was coming along nicely.

"Cupcake, where do you want these boxes stashed?"

"Mom, let me worry about it. Why don't you go ahead home? I'm okay."

"I want to make sure my baby is taken care of. I'll stay the night."

Moments like this Kara wished Dr. Jones was a fly on the wall to see that her and her mother's relationship was in a good space. When it was really time to be a loving family, the two of them could manage just fine.

"Thanks, Mom, but really. I'm okay. Go home."

"Okay, okay. You're my only baby, so you know I worry."

"I know you do, but really I've been so cooped up in that hospital room with people coming in and out that I would love a few days of alone time," Kara told her. "I've fallen behind on my case assignments, and the day of the accident I was about to begin looking into Daddy's murder as well. Now that I'm home, I'm anxious to get a head start on his old case."

Her mother froze from gathering her things. "Why are you looking into your father's murder?"

"Because"—Kara put down the folder she'd taken out of one of the boxes of case files—"it's coming up on the twentieth anniversary of his death and I'm having nightmares again. My therapist recommends that I must find peace with his death and the only way for me to do that is to solve his murder. I need to know what was going on in Daddy's life at that time."

"Oh, no, sugar. Now I'm worried. I don't want you stirring up old demons. What if whoever killed your dad finds out and comes after you? I can't bear the idea of losing you too."

"Mom, I'm a trained professional. I can handle anything thrown at me."

"Your dad used to think he was indestructible as well, and we see what happened to him." Kara limped over to her mother placing a kiss on her forehead. "And look at you now, barely able to walk. You're not indestructible either. You will do good to remember that."

"I know, Mom. Please don't worry. I'll be careful. I promise."

"Please sit down and get off that foot."

Kara took her advice. Her foot was beginning to pain her and she didn't want to risk reinjuring herself. It was not lost on her that her mother was subliminally trying to change the subject, however.

"You do realize that we're going to have to talk about the day Daddy died?" Kara watched her mother intently, seeing her mother's face scrunch up into one of distaste.

"You know I never talk about your father."

"I know, and that's a problem for me. I think that's why at times it seems as if our relationship has been strained. I just want to know what happened that day. I remember he called the house but you wouldn't let me speak to him. Why?"

"It was for your own good that you didn't speak to him. He didn't have anything to say."

"See, that's what I'm saying. What does that mean? I was five. All I wanted to do was talk to him, hear his voice. Why is that a bad thing?"

"Your father is not who you thought he was. Now I'm going to have to insist that you drop it." Kara's normally pleasant mother had turned to stone.

"No, I will not drop it," Kara responded angrily. "You're beginning to get me upset." Her voice was rising.

Kara's mother grabbed her purse indignantly. "I'm not dealing with this today. We buried your father a long time ago. I will not rehash his murder for anyone. Not even you. Call me if you need me to cook you some food or something, but if you need to talk about your father's death, don't call me for that. I can't and won't be of service to you." She stormed out of Kara's house and down the concrete stairs.

She's hiding something. Kara's training in law enforcement told her that her mother was holding back viable information. She understood that speaking about her father's death could be difficult, but that was surely no reason to have an attitude and storm out of the house. Something was definitely going on. Kara was sure of it, and she was determined to get to the bottom of the situation—but not before she combed through Ryan's case files. That was her first priority with his parole hearing approaching and her being in the hospital for over a month.

She hated that she had been given this case. She wanted to put it and Ryan behind her forever.

"Jim Schwartz, the coach from the Detroit Lions, has been in contact with my coach."

"Oh my gosh, that's so good, baby." While she was training for the academy, Ryan was hell-bent on being in the NFL, and she was proud of him for having a dream and working toward it.

"I know. I'm trying to decide if I should finish this last year of school or go into the draft."

"What does your heart tell you to do? You know I will support any decision you make," Kara told him as they watched the Ravens play Dallas at the bar in Fridays by George Washington University.

"It's telling me to enter the draft."

"Very awesome. Let's go Lions, hopefully," Kara cheered.

Ryan leaned over the table to kiss Kara's full lips. *"Have I ever told you how sexy you are when you're so supportive?"* he whispered in her ear, playfully nipping at her lobe. *"Let's get out of here."*

"Let's." Kara immediately stood, happily anticipating what awaited her for the rest of the evening.

"I'm driving; you've had a little too much to drink tonight." She reached for Ryan's keys.

Ryan happily obliged handing her the keys to his pick-up truck. *"You've thrown back a few yourself."*

"I'm in much better shape than you are though."

"Touché."

"So you're really serious about entering the draft?"

"I am."

"This is so exciting." Kara frowned, touching his knee. *"But I'm going to miss you."*

"Don't miss me yet. We still have to see where I'm going to end up."

Kara turned to gaze into his eyes. *"I know, but you know wherever you go, I have to stay here while I complete my training."*

"You have nothing to worry abou—watch out!"

Kara returned her attention to the road, just as she drove over something that forced the car to bounce heavily up and down on the road.

"Shit. What was that?" Her eyes were wide open in fear and horror as she stopped the car.

"A kid," Ryan whispered as he unlatched his seatbelt and exited the car simultaneously. Jogging back to the unmoving lump, Ryan frantically searched for a pulse.

"He's not breathing. We have to call 911."

"No, no, no." Kara shook her head back and forth. *"This cannot be happening."*

"Kara, relax; it was an accident," Ryan tried unsuccessfully to reassure her. *"We'll get through this."*

"I wasn't looking at the road; it's negligence. I hit someone, no, no, no." She bent over as a wave of vomit exited her mouth onto the asphalt.

Ryan took out his cell. "There's been an accident. Please send an ambulance. I hit a kid riding his bike and he's not breathing. Send someone fast." As Ryan hung up the phone, he told Kara, "This is the story: I was driving; the kid is in all black. I didn't see him. We were going the speed limit he appeared out of nowhere."

Kara's tear-streaked face stared at Ryan in bewilderment. "But I was driving."

"I know, but you can't have this on your record if you want to be a detective."

"We have to tell the truth," Kara insisted. "I won't be part of a lie. I did this, and I will own up to it."

"Too late, I've already told dispatch I did it," Ryan spoke with finality as the flashing lights in the distance indicated the ambulance and police would be arriving soon.

I owe him. Kara pulled more files out of the box. Ryan had sacrificed the most that night. He'd lost his football career. Once the police smelled the alcohol on his breath that night, they'd concluded that he was drunk driving and sentenced him to six years for vehicular manslaughter under the influence of alcohol. That was a hefty price to pay for a crime one didn't commit.

Sighing as she opened the files, Kara began reviewing the evidence from that night wondering what new development had taken place.

Awakened a few hours later by the sound of glass breaking, Kara chastised herself for falling asleep over the files. The painkillers the doctors had her on were a doozy.

Where is my gun? She groaned inwardly. She'd left her service revolver unsecured on her nightstand in her bedroom where the sound of the broken window had been heard. *You are such an idiot, Kara.*

Removing the foot brace that protected her broken toe, she moved at a cat's pace in tune with the shadows. The one advantage she had was knowing her house better than whoever may be in it. Taking the stairs one at a time, she listened as much as she moved. Experienced in the hunting of prey, Kara waited patiently for another sound to be heard from her room. Hearing only silence, she moved cautiously toward the bedroom, ignoring the pained protests her body was making, with her entire stance in attack mode. Clearing each doorway she passed, she was on high alert.

Peeping inside her bedroom she could see the broken glass on the floor, and shadows jumping in the moonlight, but nothing seemed to be out of place except a bouquet of stark-white roses on her nightstand where her revolver used to sit. *They have my gun. Now I have to report it to my unit. This is no good. My captain is going to kill me. Damn.*

"You really stuck your foot in this one, huh, Kay A.?"

Kara couldn't resist smiling, happy that Kyle had come over to fix her window.

"I hope not." Kara sat on the edge of the bed as she watched him insert the new window pane. "But it definitely looks bad."

"What's going on Kay A.? I go out of town for a few

weeks and to get me back here you have someone try to run you over, get a number of broken bones, and get your house broken into." He tipped his head in her direction smiling. "A simple phone call saying you missed me and couldn't live without me another minute would have sufficed. I would have been back home on the first thing smoking."

"Ha ha. I see you are full of jokes today." Kara returned his easy smile.

Kyle Whitlock, her partner in crime. She had been missing him while he was away on vacation. He was the one male on her team that had embraced her when she'd been newly assigned to the Criminal Investigation Unit. Kyle made it a point to treat her as an equal, and she loved that about him.

"Seriously, Kay A., talk to me. Who do you think is trying to hurt you?"

"I don't know." Kara was grateful for his concern. She knew Kyle cared for her. "I keep replaying that accident in my head. I saw it happening. It was this surreal feeling, you know? I was sitting there watching the whole thing unfold before my eyes. Two SUVs, one blocked me in the front and the other rammed me from the back. Luckily I was able to radio it in just before impact."

"I'm glad you were thinking quick on your feet." Kyle looked up at the ceiling that was in dire need of a paint job. "I should have been there with you. I'm your partner. It's my job to have your back at all times."

"Hey, Whitlock, don't beat yourself up about it. It's not

your job to babysit me. Come on. I'm a big girl. I got this." Kara picked up a pillow off the bed and threw it at him, hitting him square in the back of his head. Throwing her head back she laughed hard. It was good to have Kyle home.

"Hey, quit it." He ducked after the fact anticipating another pillow following the first. "Do you want me to drop this thing?" Kara continued laughing.

Kyle braced the glass on the wall, coming toward Kara with a determined look on his face. "You're still laughing, huh? Well I'ma give you something to laugh about." He wiggled his fingers as he approached and began tickling her.

"Oh my God. Stop it," Kara managed to squeeze out in between breaths as she laughed uncontrollably. "Please, Kyle. Please stop."

"Not until you apologize."

"I'm sorry, I'm sorry!" she screamed at the top of her lungs. "My ribs, they can't take this torture."

"I forgot about your ribs." He instantly released her. "That will teach you to throw pillows at me," he said as he released her, kissing her on her forehead before he retrieved the glass from the wall to insert it in the frame.

Kara sat up, grateful he had stopped tickling her. Her ribs were still tender, and the tickling hurt like hell, even though she was having fun.

"So, how was your trip?"

"It was interesting, to say the least. Beach, water, booze." He paused, turning to look in her eyes as if unsure of what to say next. "I missed you," he uttered after a beat.

Kara felt herself blushing. Kyle had that effect on her with his Mario Lopez good looks. She knew they had a chemistry between them, but she'd always ignored it out of respect for Jason. Now there was no Jason, but Kyle didn't need to know that just yet.

"I missed you too." She broke his gaze first, suddenly uncomfortable, clearing her throat. "So how long do you think fixing that window is going to take?"

"Shouldn't be too long. You trying to kick me out already?" He sounded slightly offended.

"Don't be silly. Of course not," she said as she watched the way his white tank top stretched across the muscles on his heavily tanned back. *It's been so long, maybe just this once.* Shaking her head as soon as the thought crossed her mind, she stood up from the bed.

"Would you like some water?" She needed to get out of this room that was rapidly filling with heat, and it sure wasn't from the sun outside.

"That would be great. Thanks."

"Coming right up."

TEN

"IF YOU DON'T GET AWAY FROM ME, I SWEAR I WILL SHOOT you." Kara had finally healed enough from her wounds to make it back into the office. She was in the lunchroom enjoying her peanut butter and jelly sandwich, when Misty came and sat at her table placing such a distaste in her mouth that she was no longer hungry.

"You wouldn't dare," came the undignified reply.

"Try me." Kara stared Misty straight in the eyes without flinching, wanting her to understand that she meant exactly what she was saying.

"Don't be this way. Please, let's talk. Let me explain. I owe you that much. Please," Misty pleaded mercifully.

"You have five minutes." Kara pointedly glanced at her watch. "Go."

Misty sat in the chair across from Kara. "I want to apologize."

"Apology not accepted," came Kara's bored response. "Next."

"Please don't be this way. Jason and I are very sorry."

Maybe it was the use of her and Jason's name in the same sentence, together as an item. Maybe it was the cookie-cutter way Misty thought all would be well with a simple apology. Kara couldn't be sure which pushed her over the edge, but pushed she was.

"Let me see if I have this right." If Misty wanted to put on a show, Kara was going to deliver what she wanted. "You sit there offering me an apology for marrying my ex-fiancé a mere two weeks after we break up and have the nerve to have it published in the society section of the newspaper. You, who was supposed to be my friend, who must have secretly been seeing Jason behind my back in order to get married so quickly, want me to forgive you." Kara gave a sarcastic laugh. "Did I miss anything?"

Misty shook her head.

"Well at least you're honest, even if your mother didn't raise you right." Kara leaned in close over the table. "Exactly how long did you date *my* fiancé behind my back?"

"See, that's just it, we didn't date that long. It's something that neither one of us is proud of. We just knew we had to be together."

"How long?" Kara persisted.

"Three months."

"Three months and you're married already?" Kara was beside herself. She'd dated Jason for four years before they'd become engaged.

"You think we should have invited Misty on this vacation? I feel so bad that she doesn't have a date." Kara relaxed in Jason's arms as they lay on the chaise together, bodies interlocked on the hotel balcony, enjoying the view of the waves in the ocean.

"You worry too much. Misty will be fine. She's over there having a good time. Look." Jason pointed toward the beach.

Kara looked in the direction Jason was pointing and

smiled. Misty was the life of the party. There were guys surrounding her as she danced for them. She loved being the center of attention. A pint-size Brittany Spears lookalike, if you will, with curly red hair. Most men would love a woman like Misty. Kara often wondered why she remained single.

"You want to go down to the beach?" Jason asked.

"No, you go ahead. I'ma stay up here and take a little nap."

"Alright. I'll go and save Misty from the vultures."

"Okay. Have fun, baby. Come for me in about an hour."

"Will do, my soon-to-be missus." Jason kissed the top of Kara's head. "I love you."

"I love you too."

"It began in Maui, didn't it?" Kara began fitting the pieces to the puzzle together.

Misty dropped her head.

"You slept with Jason on the very weekend he proposed to me in Maui?" Her voice rose significantly.

"Kara, we honestly never expected it to happen. I was drunk, Jason was drunk. You were asleep." Misty's voice trailed off.

"Did it occur to you that I might wake up? That's why he was late waking me up from my nap. It's all coming back to me. When we got back from vacation he began working all of those late nights. I'm thinking he wants to make extra money before we start planning the wedding."

Kara was wounded. "And the whole time he was planning a wedding with you. And nowhere in there did the two of you think I should know anything?"

"I suggested we sit down and speak with you together, but Jason insisted he should do it alone."

Kara placed her hand on her neck as she began massaging the mounting tension she felt there and stared up at the ceiling wishing she were anywhere but here. *Maybe I should have taken a few more days off from work. I'm not up to dealing with this nonsense right now.*

"When did you start planning your wedding?"

"Right after we returned from Maui. We both knew we wanted to be together forever. It was magical. The only issue . . ." Misty's voice trailed off again as she remembered.

"So, I see you down here enticing all these guys."

"I am doing no such thing." Misty laughed.

"You definitely are, and I find it very attractive."

"What? Are you serious? You can't find anything about me attractive. Where is Kara?" Misty looked around the beach hoping to catch a glimpse of her friend.

"She's napping, and I do find you attractive."

"Please don't tell me that. Kara is my friend, and I really don't want there to be any, you know, friction between the two of us. I love her. She's like the sister I always wanted but never had."

"I love Kara too. But where is she? She just left us

down here to fend for ourselves. So fend we shall."

Misty led the way. "Come on, let's go to the bar and get you some water. You're obviously drunk, and I don't want to start taking you too seriously."

"Yeah, let's go have some drinks, not water. That's something I would love to do," Jason said as he watched Misty lead the way in her string bikini, his eyes mesmerized by what he was taking in. Misty in all her freshly toned glory. Uh oh, I may be in trouble.

"We are entirely too drunk—oh my gosh. How many drinks have we had?" Misty hadn't been a responsible adult by allowing Jason to have more drinks while they sat at the bar for the last two hours.

"Entirely too many," Jason responded. "Come on," he said as he took out his credit card to pay the bill. Let me walk you back to your room.

"Okay. I think that's a good idea. I'm starting to get little woozy."

Once they returned to Misty's room, Jason was loath to leave her there by herself.

"Would it be a bad idea for me to come in?"

"I don't know, Jason. Do you think that's a really good idea?"

"Probably not. But I can't resist the urge to be with you right now."

"I feel the same way," Misty told him as she reached up and grabbed him by his shirt. "Come on in."

When Jason returned to the room later that night, Kara was up brushing her hair.

"Well hello, my sexy mister. I missed you." Kara leaned up on her tiptoes to kiss Jason's swollen lips. "Did you and Misty have a good time hanging out together while I took my nap?"

"Yeah, we did," Jason's told her, unsure of how to proceed. He was feeling extremely guilty about what had transpired between him and Misty, but yet he couldn't tell Kara what went down. He chose to continue with his regularly scheduled programming.

"You have to get dressed. I have a surprise planned for you," he told Kara.

She squealed with glee. "A surprise. How exciting. Okay, I'll be just a moment."

Moments later, once Kara had put herself together, Jason guided her outside to the bonfire he had planned for them. Once there he had ladies come over and dance for them. Their own special, private luau. She was so caught up in the festivities, Kara was surprised when Jason grabbed her hand and dropped down on one knee.

"Kara Anthony, you are the love of my life and I cannot imagine forever without you in it. Will you marry me?"

Kara's eyes bulged big and bright as she realized what was taking place.

"Oh my gosh, Jason! Absolutely yes. I would love to marry you. I cannot wait. My forever doesn't exist without you in it either." Tears streamed down her face as she was beside herself with emotion. Never did she ever think she would pull a man like Jason, and then not only pull him for a boyfriend, but also have him ask her to marry him. He

wanted her to be his wife. How amazing.

Jason's smile didn't quite reach his eyes as he placed the flawless diamond on her ring finger and drew her into his arms for a kiss as cheers were heard from a distance as other vacationers realized what was going on, on the hill.

Jason let Kara loose as soon as Misty arrived at their spot.

"Misty, you missed it." Kara's face was alive with merriment. "Jason has asked me to marry him. Isn't that amazing? This adorable man wants to be my husband."

"That sure is something," Misty responded behind a forced grin. "Aren't you the lucky one?"

Still too excited to hear the censorship in Misty's tone, Kara was on cloud nine.

"This has been the most amazing night of my life, and I will never forget it, Jason. I love you so much."

"I love you too. For always."

Later that evening after Jason had made love to Kara and put her to sleep, he snuck out of his room to go to Misty's room so they could talk. He knocked on the door and waited.

Misty opened the door pissed off.

"How could you still propose to her after what happened with me and you today?"

"What was I supposed to do? I brought her here to propose to her."

"Yeah, well, she didn't know that. You didn't have to propose to her today. What about what happened with you and I? What is that?"

"I don't know what that is." Jason sat on the bed. "What is that?" Jason asked, looking at Misty.

"I don't know. But we need to figure it out, and we need to figure it out quickly. Do you, do you really love Kara? If so then you have to tell her about tonight."

"Of course I love Kara. I never would've proposed if I didn't."

"Well then it's up to you to tell her about us or I'm going to have to do it."

"I don't want to hurt her, but I need to figure this all out in my head first."

"You know what I think, Jason?"

"No, what?"

"That you really don't want to marry Kara and you were looking for an out. That's why you slept with me."

"Is that what you really think? Why is that so?"

"Because if you really loved her and you really wanted to marry her, you never would have slept with me. Nothing would have stopped you from proposing to her and being all in love with her. You were looking for an out; I gave it to you."

Jason just stared at Misty. Maybe she had a point. He and Kara were at that stage in their relationship where it was either shit or get off the pot, as his grandfather used to say to him. He couldn't drag her on forever, so he'd done the honorable thing; but the truth was his heart wasn't in it. He and Kara had been coasting through their relationships for years now, not accomplishing anything, just being.

"You know what else I think?"

"You seem to have all the answers today, so please continue."

"I think you want to be with me. And have wanted to for a long time. I see the way you always look at me when I'm around. There's no need to deny it."

"I wasn't going to."

"Good, that's a plus on your part. Actually, I've come to like you, and I would hate for you to disappoint me so soon."

Jason laughed in spite of himself.

"Misty, is this something you really want to get started?"

"Oh yes, Jason, I absolutely want to get this started. I've been waiting for you to come around for a long time now. It's about time you saw what was right before your eyes."

"I'm going to have to talk to Kara about this at some point."

"Yes, you will. We can do it together."

"No, I think it's best if I speak to her alone. I owe her that much."

"Suit yourself. But if you need me I'm here."

"Misty, just to be clear, this doesn't mean you and I are an item. It just means Kara isn't the one for me and you and I are just having a good time."

"Jason, we'll see about that, my darling. Now take your clothes off and join me in the hot tub."

"I would love to. But I should really get back to the room before Kara wakes up."

"And so it begins already. When are you going to let her know again? I definitely hope sooner than later."

"It will be soon, but it will take place once we are back home, not here on vacation where I just proposed to her. She was so excited. I want her to enjoy her new engagement a little before I have to break the news that is sure to devastate her. It's just too soon, and I refuse to hurt her like that."

"It's sure to devastate her either way. The longer you prolong the inevitable, the harder it will be for her to accept."

"I will do it in my own time," Jason said with finality. *Misty wasn't going to coerce him into anything else this evening. He was going to handle Kara the way he thought was best.*

"Have a good night, Misty. See you tomorrow before we head off to the airport."

"You sure I can't persuade you to stay?" Misty tried enticing Jason once more, dropping her robe to the floor.

Taking in her nudity by the moonlight coming from the window, Jason felt his resolve weakening.

"Five minutes won't hurt." He changed his mind as he pulled his shirt off, picking Misty up off the floor as she straddled her bare legs around him and they made their way to the hot tub.

"The only issue was me, right?" Kara couldn't think straight; she was going to lose it at any moment. "Say it!" she demanded of Misty.

"Yes. You were the only obstacle in our way."

"You were supposed to be my friend. This is about to be the shortest wedding on record."

"Why do you say that?"

Kara calmly drew her newly assigned revolver. "Because I'm about to kill you."

Misty kicked back from the table, ducking to the floor and drawing her own weapon, pointing it at Kara's head. "Kara, I understand that you're upset, but put the gun down now. Don't make me hurt you."

"Hurt me?" Kara laughed hysterically. "I'm already hurt. You've accomplished that. But I'm going to shoot you. Yes"—Kara nodded her head—"that will make me feel better."

Forced to the ground by two officers, Kara had been so engrossed in her speech she hadn't heard them approach.

"What are you doing, Detective?" one of the black-and-whites asked her as he disarmed her of her weapon and pulled out his cuffs. "We're going to have to detain you." Kara barely heard the words as she stared at Misty, wishing she could do her bodily harm.

"Explain to me why one of my valued detectives had to be detained?" The captain's brash tone caused Kara to flinch, no more than five minutes after she'd been cuffed.

Kara looked at the floor tile, this not being one of her proudest moments.

"Captain, we all go through things."

Grateful to her partner for stepping up, Kara said

nothing.

"Hey, Whitlock, when I want your answer I'll ask for it. Let Anthony respond for herself. Unless all of a sudden her mouth doesn't work."

"My mouth works just fine, Captain," Kara responded softly.

"I thought it might." He stood in front of her with his arms crossing his chest. "What happened in that lunchroom today?"

"It's personal," Kara mumbled.

"No, it's not personal. Nothing is personal when you put other people's lives in danger," the captain pointed out to Kara. "But personal or otherwise, I am placing you on administrative leave with pay pending an investigation. We already have your weapon. Turn in your badge and get home safely."

Kara had never felt so dismissed in her life. Standing, she pulled her badge out of her pocket and placed it on the captain's desk, retreating from his office with no further words. There was no need to plead her case. She was lucky they hadn't put her in a holding cell for her actions. She was still in shock herself that she would lose it to that extent.

"Hey, Kay A., wait up."

Kara stopped walking allowing Kyle the opportunity to catch up to her.

"What's going on? I thought you and Misty were friends?"

Pushing through the glass doors that led outside, Kara

shielded her eyes from the sunlight.

"Yeah, well, you thought wrong." The two walked in silence to the black sedan they drove together. "Kyle, I'm sorry. I didn't mean that. Today has been difficult."

Kyle pulled her into his arms. "It's going to be okay. You know you can always talk to me."

Kara returned his embrace.

"Misty and Jason are married."

Kyle pulled away. "You lie."

"Come on, Kyle, you know I wouldn't lie about something like this. Not this serious."

Kyle shook his head. "And when did this happen?"

"About a month ago."

"Gee, I go on one vacation and the sky falls. Is my name still Kyle Whitlock?"

Kara gave a slight smile in spite of her dire circumstances. "Tell me about it. All it takes is one vacation to change everything," Kara echoed.

"I can't believe you pulled a gun on Misty." Kyle laughed as they entered the sedan, with him behind the wheel. "Can't believe I missed that. I would have given my future firstborn to be in that lunchroom today."

"She deserved it." Kara felt no remorse for drawing her weapon. She knew she wasn't going to shoot Misty, or at least she liked to think she wouldn't have, that hopefully she was better than that and that *her* mother had raised her right.

"I'm neutral."

Kara punched Kyle in the arm.

"No you're not. You're team Kara, buddy."

Kyle chuckled, "Team Kara it is. I'm fonder of you anyway." He grinned as he drove Kara home.

The first thing Kara noticed when they pulled up was that her front door was lying on the ground, her house open to whoever wanted to enter. *What in the world?*

"Stay here while I check this out." Kyle had barely cut the car off before he had jogged to her door.

"I am not staying in this car. This is *my* house." Kara exited the car and crept behind Kyle.

"Stay close to me," Kyle told her rather than argue. "Without a weapon, you are vulnerable."

"I am well aware. Okay, partner, lead the way." Kara followed on Kyle's heels as they entered her house.

Ten minutes later the entire house had been cleared and was completely empty.

"This is getting ridiculous. Whoever is doing this is intent on damaging my house, forcing me to shell out more and more money."

"Yeah, I'm about to start charging you as your handyman." He laughed.

"Kyle, could you be serious for a moment? This is not funny. Someone is stalking me and willing to hurt me."

"I'm sorry Kay A.," Kyle immediately relented. "I don't take this or your safety lightly. I was only trying to lighten the mood."

Kara took in the broken door on the ground. "What am I going to do? I can't stay here without a door."

"Stay with me. I have the space. And this way I'll be

able to keep an eye on you and keep you safe until we figure out who or what is trying to bring you harm."

Kara eyed Kyle suspiciously. "I don't know if that is such a good idea."

"I promise to be on my best behavior." Kyle placed his hand over his heart in an attempt to show his sincerity. "Scout's honor."

"Okay, maybe for a little while. It will be nice to feel safe for once."

"You'll definitely be safe with me."

Kara wondered just which safe he was referencing as she packed a few items to bring with her to Kyle's house.

ELEVEN

"WHY WERE YOU BOTHERING HER ANYWAY? I THOUGHT I TOLD you to stay away from Kara. There was absolutely no reason for you to approach her about anything."

"She pulled a gun on me, and you're giving me the lecture? You have some nerve."

"No, Misty, you have some nerve. Leave Kara alone. Now she's on administrative leave because of you."

"No, she's on administrative leave because she pulled a gun on me. I don't believe this. I'm the victim, and you're standing there taking her side."

"You make it easy to take her side when you're running around acting like a raving lunatic." Jason was beyond himself with anger. Leave it to Misty to disrupt his life even more. She was a mistake. Their marriage was a sham.

"I've had reporters buzzing me all day about what happened at the station."

"I don't care. Tell them to mind their business," was Misty's retort. She could care less about reporters contacting Jason. Her life had been in danger and her own husband was acting like it was no big deal.

"Well you should care. I cannot have negative press. My businesses will suffer. It would do you some good to act respectable."

Misty's mouth dropped open in disbelief. "I am not the one that caused the problem here."

"The fact that you can't see that you *are* the problem speaks volumes and lets me know that you lack the maturity to see the error in your ways."

"So, I'm immature now. Is that it?"

Jason ran his fingers through his hair. "Look, it's been a long day for both of us. I'm sorry that you had a gun pulled on you. However, in all fairness, you provoked a fight and you aren't some damsel in distress. You are more than capable of defending yourself, as you did. To play the victim card is a bit much, even for you. Now, I'm done with this conversation. I'll see you tomorrow. I'ma book a hotel tonight. I can't be around you tonight."

"You can't just leave. Every time something goes bad with Kara and me, you can't just bail. At some point, you are going to have to take a stand and support your wife."

"My *wife*, and I use the term loosely, needs to learn how to conduct herself accordingly. If you made it a point to do that, we wouldn't even be having this conversation right now, now would we?"

"You know what? You're an asshole. I can't believe I signed up for this."

"Yeah, well that makes two of us. I'll be back tomorrow." Jason picked up his briefcase and exited the house that he paid a $5,000 mortgage on every month. He was intent on getting as far away from his new bride as one man could possibly get without fleeing the state.

TWELVE

"HOW HAVE THINGS BEEN GOING SINCE THE LAST TIME WE met?"

Kara lay on the black chaise with her eyes closed. "Horrible. I may need to be on some kind of suicide watch. An hour just isn't long enough, Doc."

"I can clear my schedule for you," came Dr. Jones's patient reply.

"Will you? That would be wonderful."

"Sure. I'll be with you in a few minutes." Dr. Jones made a few calls and then returned her attention to Kara. She knew she shouldn't play favorites with her clients, but Kara had held a special place in her heart since she'd been fourteen: the rebellious teen she'd helped shape and mold into the woman she was today. She took pride in that.

"Okay. You have my undivided attention. Start at the beginning."

"Someone is trying to kill me."

"Why do you feel that way?"

"I don't *feel* that way. This isn't some sort of optical illusion or a mirage. It is something that is really happening. It's because of the events that have taken place recently back-to-back. There is little doubt in my mind that someone intends me harm."

"Tell me about what you have been experiencing."

"The last time I left your office, I stopped by the cleaners to get my clothes, and on the way home I was waiting at a stop sign, and one SUV blocked me in while another approached me from the back and rammed me. I spent a couple of weeks in the hospital."

"My goodness." Barbara was perplexed. "Why didn't you contact me about this?"

"I don't know. It was—" Kara paused "—it was just so much happening. I didn't even think about it. Yesterday I was placed on administrative leave from my job."

"What?" It was rare that Barbara was shocked by something a client said. But Kara was usually on the straight and narrow. She couldn't imagine what she must have done in order to be placed on administrative leave.

"Okay, we really do need to talk." Barbara removed her glasses and stared at Kara. "Let's begin with the accident. Did you tell the police?"

"Yes. I was able to radio it in before it happened."

"Are they investigating?"

"Of course they are. They are having a difficult time finding witnesses, however, which is hard for me to believe because the area by my house generally stays busy. There is a lot of foot traffic." Kara opened her eyes gazing at the ceiling, noticing for the first time that there was a mural of an African art piece by LaShun Beal, who she was a huge fan of and was able to recognize his art immediately. *How have I missed that all these years?* That tidbit of information made her like Dr. Jones just a little bit more.

"The mural is new." Barbara saw her staring at the ceiling quizzically.

"I was wondering how I missed that all these years. I can't be that unaware." Kara laughed. "But I just don't believe there is no way someone didn't see something," she said, jumping right back into the conversation about her accident.

"Why do you think no one is stepping forward?"

"The same reason people never step forward in an investigation. Because they're afraid," Kara stated plainly. "That's usually the reason people don't come forward with information. Either they are afraid, or they are involved."

It pained Kara to think that her neighbors could have been a part of her accident in some way. Now she knew she couldn't trust anyone.

"How do you feel?"

"I feel betrayed, Barbara. I feel betrayed in all aspects of my life."

"Explain," Dr. Jones encouraged.

"My house has been broken into twice. First my bedroom window gets smashed. Then I come home on the day I've been placed on administrative leave, and the front door to my house is laying on the ground."

"Where are you staying right now? I hope not at your house." Barbara was genuinely concerned.

"No. I'm crashing at Kyle's until things settle down a little bit. Attacks on my life and frequent break-ins are a cause for me to slow down a little."

"Good. You have to be careful. I know you're a bigtime detective now, but I still see the teenager with pink and black hair, and a spiked collar around her neck, crying out for clarity and understanding with a heart of gold begging to be loved."

Kara smiled. "Seems so long ago. I was such a mess. Thank you for helping fix me."

"You're fixing yourself, present tense. We are all a

work in progress until the day we leave this earth. All I did was help guide you in the right direction," Barbara corrected her.

"Either way, I thank you."

Barbara smiled. "How are things with Kyle? I know he's your partner, but living together introduces a whole other component."

"Yes, it does." Kara laughed. "Kyle and I are good. He gives me my space. He allows me the run of the basement, and I've turned it into a quaint little apartment. We mostly see each other in the mornings only, because he still has a job to report to, while I'm stuck trying to occupy my time."

"What are you doing to occupy your time?"

"Before I was sent home on leave, my captain gave me a case to follow up on. So I'm boning up on that at the moment."

"Good. Try to stay busy. An idle mind is the devil's playground."

Kara smiled. Dr. Jones had been telling her that since she was a teenager. Part of the reason she felt her mother had been so gung-ho about her therapist is because of her religious roots. Kara's mother believed in church and reading her Bible faithfully, which is why Kara couldn't understand her mother's behavior when it came to the topic of her father. The next time she caught an attitude Kara was going to say, "Now is that what Jesus would do?" just to see her mother's reaction.

"My mother won't discuss the day my father passed away," Kara blurted out. "She's so grief-stricken that she immediately shuts down if I mention him. I need to talk about him to heal. It seems like she doesn't understand that or doesn't want to understand. She is hell-bent on him never being discussed."

"So why not seek answers elsewhere?" Dr. Jones suggested. "While your mom is a great woman, she's not the only pool of information you can pull from. Don't focus so much of your energy there. It will only sour you and your mother's relationship, and the two of you have come such a long way from your younger years."

Kara sat in bewilderment at Barbara's statement. *Why didn't I think of that? What kind of Detective am I, that I can't think of simple solutions like this one? Of course I can ask other people about my father. Of course I can.*

"Dr. Jones, you are the absolute best." Her face filled with glee. "May I hug you?"

Barbara stood. "Of course you can, honey." Kara embraced her. In some ways, she thought of Dr. Jones as more of a mother than her own. She was more understanding and had been in her corner for eleven years.

"Thank you." Kara closed her eyes. "You're the kind of mother I always wanted."

"I'm always here if you need me. You know that." Barbara sat back in her chair. "You have my number, call me anytime."

"Will do." Kara was much encouraged. She had a new angle for discovering information about her father and she was anxious to get started.

THIRTEEN

"WHAT DO YOU WANT FROM MY LIFE? WHY KEEP COMING here?"

"Tell me about Sophie."

"What?"

"Sophie, that's your wife's name, right?" Kara quipped. She was back in North Carolina at the correctional facility, demanding answers from Ryan. In her exhausting research reading pity session that took place in her small basement apartment at Kyle's house, she had come across some interesting information in Ryan's file, such as Sophie.

"Yes, my wife's name is Sophie," Ryan acknowledged. "I don't see why that's relevant to you though. Why do you care who I'm married to?"

"Oh, it wouldn't, except Sophie happens to be the daughter of my captain. Are you insane?" Kara was trying to put the pieces of the puzzle together. She had never met her captain's daughter because she had grown up and settled as an adult in North Carolina with her mother.

"She's your captain's daughter, so what?" Ryan shrugged, wondering why Kara was reacting this way. "That makes me insane how? You need to be more clear in what you're saying."

"No, it's not a so what. Something is going on here. Everything is entirely too circumstantial for there not to be."

Ryan continued to stare at her like she was crazy.

"Hear me out." Kara began whispering, "Why would

my captain insist that I be on your case, the case that happens to involve his son-in-law? The same case I testified on so many years ago and should not be working on right now?"

Ryan shrugged again. "You're the detective, not me. I shouldn't even be speaking to you."

"Okay, let's get something straight, because this little guilt trip you try to put me on is unjust." Kara pointed a finger at Ryan. "You're the one that took the blame for running over that kid. I never told you to do that. You sealed your fate."

"Don't try it. You left me at the scene. You could have stayed and at least been by my side. You left me, then came back and pretended that you saw the whole thing go down and gave that bogus story about me looking like I was under the influence and that you had seen my car swerving back and forth over the street lines. You're the reason they tested me for alcohol."

Kara was beside herself with anger. "You are so delusional. They would have tested your blood and alcohol levels anyway. You reeked of alcohol."

"You have no right to be angry." Ryan stood up. "None. I took the rap for you and you got to live your normal life." His face was red with anger. "I have every right to be upset. You left me to rot in here. After I got sentenced and sent down here you never visited, not one time, until a few weeks ago when you were assigned to my case. No letters, nothing."

"I thought it would have been bad for my career, but

that doesn't change that I loved you."

Ryan shook his head in disbelief. "No, I loved you. You see what I did for love. That's why I'm here. We could have survived this together. If the role had been reversed, I would have been here for you. I'm glad your career meant so much to you. You took up with that new guy and I never heard from you. Then you come here with your high-and-mighty attitude demanding answers. Well let me say this to you. You're dead to me. Don't come back. I never want to see you again. Seeing how I'm bad for your career and all."

Signaling the guard, Ryan was escorted out of the room as Kara sat there. *Well that went over well, Anthony. Now he doesn't want to see you again and you didn't get any of the questions you came to ask answered.*

~ ~ ~

"Long day?"

Letting the steam from the hot water relax her muscles, Kara with closed eyes simply nodded yes in response to Kyle's question.

"Want to talk about it?" he asked, leaning his tall frame against the bathroom door.

"Not really," she mumbled.

"Humor me anyway."

"How about we talk about your day instead?" She wasn't the least bit concerned about having Kyle watching her bathe. The bubbles had her completely covered, and they usually engaged in conversation during these late-night hours.

"I'd rather not. It's not the same with my partner missing in action."

"They haven't paired you with anyone else?"

"No. I asked not to be assigned a new partner. I'll wait until you return from administrative leave. How was your ride to North Carolina?" Kyle asked as he flipped the lid down and sat on top of the commode so he could talk comfortably.

Kara sighed, opening her eyes. Kyle was determined to hear about her day. He was persistent that way, which made him good at his job, but sometimes could tick her nerves just a little.

"It didn't go well at all. Ryan banned me from speaking to him again."

"You need to fix this thing between you two." Kyle was the only other person that knew the true story about her and Ryan's past. One drunken night long ago when they'd first been partnered up she'd let it slip in a binge of booze and confessions.

"I don't know how. He's so angry with me."

"You're both to blame for the situation, but from the outside looking in his anger comes from you abandoning him, not so much the case itself."

Kara was shocked. Kyle had hit the nail on the head. "That's exactly what he said, in so many words." Kara gazed at Kyle through lowered eyelids. "Do you honestly think I abandoned him?"

"Didn't you?" Kyle asked. "He takes your bid for you,

you don't write him, you don't visit, you get a new man. You moved on with your career and your life. There was no room for Ryan."

Kara shook her head in disbelief. "That sounds terrible. I can't believe I'm that shallow of a person."

"I don't believe you're shallow. You were just dealt a shitty hand in life and rather than take on more bad, you chose to distance yourself from it. You went into survival mode. There's nothing wrong with protecting yourself from pain, but you have to understand there is someone sitting at the other end who didn't have the luxury of continuing their life. Ryan is entitled to his feelings," Kyle, always the candidly honest and diplomatic one, pointed out to her.

"Geez. I'm a horrible person. I did abandon him. My Ryan. How could I do that to a man I was in love with?"

"You were looking out for your best interest. Don't beat yourself up about it, just figure out what you can do to fix it."

"Thank you for being so honest. I needed it." Kara was grateful for Kyle's outlook.

"Only way I know how to be."

"I did find out an interesting fact when I was going through Ryan's records." Kara was anxious to change the topic from her bad deeds. "Ryan is married to Sophie. Sophie is Captain Harris's daughter."

"I know, I met her today."

Kara sat up erect in the bathtub, shocked. "What? But how?"

Kyle motioned for Kara to cover up as he respectfully

averted his eyes from her bare pert breasts. Hastily lowering herself back into the water, Kara waited patiently for Kyle's answer, too curious for his answer to be embarrassed by her nudity.

"She came to the station today to meet with Captain H," Ryan stated matter-of-factly.

"How is it that I've never seen Sophie one time in the five years I've been a part of the unit? Then the one time I'm placed on administrative leave and working on Ryan's case, she pops up?" Kara narrowed her eyes. "Something about her and this case is fishy to me. I don't know what it is yet, but something is not right. I was just telling Ryan today that there are too many circumstantial events happening so close to this case."

"Well, Detective, it's your case now. Figure it out."

"I'm going to do exactly that," Kara stated. "Can you hand me a towel, please? I have work to do."

FOURTEEN

THE WINDING DOWN OF TIME IS A BEAUTIFUL THING. IT IS THE flowers in full bloom during the summer returning to the ground from where they came in winter. The same as the death of any living creature: from ashes to ashes and dust to dust. Dust is nearing, and I am ready. I love that my pretty detective feels comfortable and safe now. She has stopped looking over her shoulder. And thus, has left me room to enter.

FIFTEEN

THE LAST FEW WEEKS THAT SHE'D BEEN AT KYLE'S HAD BEEN peaceful. Preparing for brunch with her mother at Front Page in the city before she headed down to the station at District Seven to do further investigating, Kara had been praying all morning that they hadn't heard about her being placed on administrative leave, so she could get answers to the questions she sought.

Opening the front door, a feeling of dread washed over her. There resting on the front step was a bouquet of white roses and a note with her name on it. Turning her head to look up and down the street, she didn't notice anything out of place. Checking the time on her watch, she saw it was twelve fifteen in the afternoon. Kyle had left around eleven thirty to go on a bike ride with his friends. Whoever had left the flowers and note had done so in a forty-five-minute time span. *I'm being watched.*

Kara retreated into the house and texted Kyle to come back home. A code red was happening. After the accident that left her sandwiched between two SUVs, she refused to take a risk by exiting the house and being exposed, putting herself in danger. Her body, while better, was not the same as before she had been in the accident. She knew another one of that magnitude was likely to kill her.

Pulling her registered 9mm out of her purse, she sat with it in her lap as she waited for Kyle's return.

Kyle came bursting through the door fifteen minutes later. "Kay A.," he screamed as he entered. "Where are you? You safe?"

"I'm over here. Yes, I'm good."

"What's wrong? You said there is a code red. I rushed home." Kyle was breathing heavily. Kara could only imagine the effort he put in on a bicycle to get home so quickly.

"I received a bouquet of flowers and a note on the front step, the same type of note and flowers that I received while I was in the hospital."

"There was nothing on the step."

"What?" Kara stood up surprised as she walked to the front door and opened it. "That can't be. They were right there." She took in the empty step, looking back at Kyle worriedly. "Honestly, Kyle, they were right on this step no more than fifteen minutes ago."

Kyle came up behind her enveloping Kara in a hug. "I believe you."

Kara had the distinct feeling that Kyle was only saying that to appease her.

"When's the last time you spoke to your therapist?" he asked softly as he rested his chin atop her hair.

Kara pulled away glaring at him. "I am not crazy. There were flowers and a note on that step."

"I wasn't insinuating that you are crazy." Kyle's patient words drifted to her ears. "All I'm saying is that you are under a lot of stress right now. And it may do you some good to speak with her."

"Cut the crap, okay? That's another way of saying, 'Kara, you're losing it,' and I am not losing it."

Kyle wisely said nothing. He knew the last few months had been extremely hard on Kara, and while she tried to act like nothing was bothering her and that she could withstand any and everything, he knew she was on the verge of a breakdown. He was concerned.

"What were you about to do today?"

"Go to brunch with Mom."

"Why not ask her to come over instead?" he suggested. "That way I can keep an eye on you and make sure nothing else happens."

"I like that idea," Kara agreed.

"Thanks for having me over, cupcake. I like this much better than a restaurant."

Kara smiled at her mother. This was their first time seeing each other since her mother stormed out of her house.

"Never a problem. You know I like spending time with you."

"Kyle keeps a nice house. Tell him I said so."

"I'll be sure to relay the message. He'll appreciate that."

"It's nice to see you've healed up nicely, since I haven't seen your face in a while."

Here we go.

"Well, Mother"—Kara's tone was tense—"you're the one that walked out of my house with an attitude. Remember?" she pointed out to her mother.

"I never live in the past, sugar. I'm about forward

movement."

Kara stared at her mother for a moment, unable to believe that she came from this woman's womb. They were as different as night and day. *I must take after my father.*

"Mom, we have to talk about Daddy," Kara stated firmly, determined to stand her ground this time, while bracing herself for an uphill battle.

Her mother sighed, "I know."

Kara's eyes widened. *Did I hear her correctly?*

"What do you want to know?"

"Everything." Kara fully intended to take advantage of this opportunity on the off chance that her mother closed the topic down again for another twenty years. Her mother had never told her tales of her father, something that she had craved her entire youth.

"Start at the beginning, Mommy." She was as giddy as a little girl.

Her mother stared off into space as if she'd left this world for a different one.

"We're pregnant!" Her deep violet eyes radiant as they gleamed in the moonlight. Her heart bursting with joy. Finally—she'd been trying to get pregnant for over a year.

"That's amazing news, Victoria," Charles beamed. Even though he'd been hesitant, he knew how much it meant to her to be a mother, and he wanted to give her that, pleased that he could.

"I've been on cloud nine all morning since I returned from the doctor's waiting for you to call. I've already got a color scheme chosen for the nursery."

Charles was genuinely happy for her, but this changed nothing about what they had spoken about.

"Victoria, we have an agreement."

"I know, Chuck, I know."

"Mom, did you hear me?" Kara raised her voice slightly, jolting her mother out of her daze.

"I'm sorry, cupcake. What did you say?"

"I asked what Daddy was like. I can't remember anymore."

"Charismatic. Very charming. Handsome as Sean Connery during his James Bond days. Very distinguished." She laughed fondly. "Lord knows I loved that man." Sadness clouded her face.

"Did he read many books, what were his interests?" Kara moved on quickly, anticipating that at any moment her mother would shut down on her.

"Oh yes," her mother gushed, "he was an avid reader. Well versed in Hemingway's novels and adventures. A fan of Edgar Allan Poe. Your father used to adore writing me poetry. I adored receiving it just as much." She blushed. "A smooth talker your father was."

Kara grinned, happy for this small insight into the life of her father that she had been robbed of knowing.

"Tell me more." She imagined herself a girl of five again sitting at her mother's knee for a bedtime story.

"The day your father re-enlisted in the army was one of the hardest days of my life. I couldn't understand why he would do it. We had a baby on the way, financially we were stable, but he always had a notion about wanting to return to serving this great country, and within a few weeks he was gone from me."

The wistfulness in her mother's tone was not lost on Kara as she reached her hand out to touch her mother's.

"He always came back, Mother."

"He did, didn't he?" Her mother's tone carried sorrow as she glanced up removing her hand from under Kara's.

Kara knew the spell was broken. Her mother had closed herself and her heart off, and it was unknown if she would ever open up again on the subject of Charles Lee Anthony.

SIXTEEN

"I DIDN'T MAKE IT UP. YOU BELIEVE ME, DON'T YOU?"

"Of course I do."

Her sure statement helped Kara sigh in relief. It was nice to be taken seriously and to have someone believe her. She knew Kyle was trying to help her, but deep down she had doubts about if he believed her story about the flowers being left on the front step or not. Dr. Jones never judged.

"Can I ask you a personal question?"

"Absolutely. You can always ask me anything."

"Why don't you have children?" Kara was curious. Barbara had such a mother's spirit.

"I had two once upon a time, but things change. Now I have one, and he is amazing. He is studying overseas in Italy for his masters." Pride and a hint of sadness were prevalent in her tone.

"Did you have girls or boys?" Kara treaded lightly.

"One of each," Barbara told her proudly, hesitantly apprehensive about the question she knew was coming next.

"May I ask what happened to your little girl?"

"She was murdered," Barbara whispered without beating around the bush. "She would have been twenty-five this year. Same age as you." She choked back the tears. She couldn't believe she was losing control of her therapy session. She was the therapist, not the client. Barbara reached for a piece of tissue off her desk and attempted to compose herself.

"I'm sorry, Dr. Jones. I had no idea." Kara was beside herself. She never intended to make her therapist cry. *Tragedy doesn't have anyone's name written on it; it affects us all.*

"It's alright." Barbara wiped her eyes. "Let's get back on topic. Tell me how things are going with your mother."

"Good. For once. She recently opened up and told me a little about my father."

"That's wonderful news," Barbara responded, happy that Kara was able to accomplish something she had fought so long to achieve. "How did you get her to come around?"

"I simply said we need to talk about him and she said okay. Really easy, just like that." Kara slapped her hands together and grinned, giving Barbara a candid display of all thirty-two of her pearly whites. "It meant the world to me, and I can tell that he was her world. She gushed about him and blushed like a school girl. I've never seen my mother look so alive."

"This is very good news, and I am happy the two of you are communicating. How is everything with you and Misty? Have you spoken to her since your administrative leave?"

"I have nothing whatsoever to say to Misty. I do believe that it is safe to say once your friend marries your fiancé and you pull a gun on her that the two of you will never be friends ever again in this lifetime."

"Kara, I see a pattern of events happening here."

Dr. Jones's comment piqued Kara's curiosity. "What sort of pattern?"

"You have a tendency to not deal with anything that hurts you. You're an emotional runner, and you can't do that in life and be healthy. You have to start bringing closure to all these wayward events that have taken place in your life."

"It's not that many," Kara began to argue.

"Yes it is. Shall we count them?" Barbara tilted her head in Kara's direction. "There is the situation with your father that is the root of your pain that you are procrastinating on dealing with. There is the problem with you and Ryan; the issue with you, Jason, and Misty; the conflict between you and your mother; the administrative leave at your job; trying to find out who is stalking you or trying to kill you. The common denominator is you. You have entirely too many loose ends. Take control of your life and deal with these matters. Change begins with you. If you want happiness, you have to fight for it. Fight for it," Barbara emphasized. "If anyone deserves happiness, you do. The next time I see you I want you to come in here with a closure story. You are a mess right now, for a lack of better words. Fix your life."

Kara lay on the chaise for a moment not uttering a word, thinking. Her therapist since forever had called her a mess. *Am I that much of a mess? I didn't realize I had this many problems. Geez, no wonder I'm at odds with everyone.*

"I am a mess," Kara agreed after a few minutes crept by with the two of them sitting in an uncomfortable silence.

"You know what's great about messes?" Barbara

cheerfully chimed in.

"No."

"They are all fixable with a little cleaning." She smiled at Kara. "It's time for you to clean house. Get rid of all this negativity. Don't block your blessings. Clean all this clutter out of your heart and mind. You will be so much better for it," Dr. Jones enthused.

Kara sighed, "It's so much."

"It is going to be an uphill battle; I won't lie to you. But you can do it. Start with what you can control right now and work your way outward. You can do this. And remember, next session you must come in here to tell me about closure on something off that long laundry list you are dragging behind you."

"I can do this," Kara said aloud, trying to convince herself.

"You can do anything you put your mind to, sweetie. Go out there and make me proud. If it gets rough, call me. I will coach you through, every step of the way."

"Thank you, Barbara. I really needed this session."

"Yes you did, and you're going to knock 'em dead. I believe in you," she said with a wink.

Kara returned the wink as she gathered her things to leave. She had a daunting task on her hands, and for the life of her, she hadn't the slightest clue of where to begin.

SEVENTEEN

"YOU'RE SUSPENDED."

"Suspended?" Kara questioned softly.

"Come on!" came Kyle's angry outburst. "Suspension, seriously?"

It was Monday morning and Captain Harris had called Kara and Kyle to his office for a meeting. "Why has my administrative leave been upgraded to suspension?"

"Misty has filed a formal complaint against you."

Kara agitatedly rubbed her eyebrow. *Misty is becoming a thorn in my side that will not dislodge itself. Now I'm suspended?*

"What does suspension entail exactly?" She needed to know the full extent of what she was dealing with.

"Considering that you're already being investigated for the lunchroom incident, this does not work well in your favor, Anthony."

"Meaning?"

"Meaning, the director called for your suspension and I support the decision. So effective immediately, you are suspended without pay pending the results of the investigation and Misty's complaint. Clean out your office before you leave. We are short on space here and will be utilizing the space in your absence."

"This is bull crap and you know it," Kyle interjected. "Everyone knows Kara was not going to shoot Misty that day. I've heard a few accounts from eyewitnesses that Misty provoked her."

The captain's face turned beet red. "Whitlock, unless you want to find yourself suspended with her, I'd advise you remember who you are and who I am. You work for me, not vice versa. I brought you here to be moral support for your partner. Show me that I shouldn't question my own judgment."

Kara was in shocked disbelief.

"Come on, Kara." Kyle stood abruptly. "You don't need this." Kara knew he was upset. Kyle never called her Kara.

"Wait a minute." Kara stood slowly to square off with the captain. "Since I'm no longer employed here for the time being, I have a question for you."

"What is it, Anthony?" The captain's condescending tone filled the quiet room like a shockwave.

"Why did you put me on the Spellman case? Especially since your daughter turns out to be Sophie Spellman, Ryan's wife. It's a personal case for you as well as me. Neither one of us should be able to touch it."

"Are you accusing me of something, Anthony?" The captain was in a full-blown rage.

"Of course not," Kara responded sweetly. "I would never do that. I was merely asking a question. I am fully aware of my place."

"As of right now you don't have a place here. Get out of my office." The captain's tone spat venom into the air.

"With pleasure." Kara refused to be intimidated. Kyle held the office door open as they made their exit.

"Way to stick it to him, Kay A."

"Not too shabby yourself, Whitlock." *My job is my life.* On the outside Kara was acting as if she were fine, but on the inside she wanted to scream out in anguish as the pair cleaned out her office and headed to the parking lot.

"I think I want to pay Misty a visit." Kara broke the silence in the car as Kyle drove them back to his place.

Kyle shifted his gaze from the road to his suspended partner. "I don't think that's a good idea. Usually I respect your right to do whatever you want, but considering all that has transpired between the two of you, I see a confrontation ending badly."

"I appreciate your concern, but I truly want to fix things with Misty. While we will never be friends again, that's a given, I do want my job back. The only way to do that is to have a sit-down with her and see if we can smooth this over."

"A mediator should be present."

"We do not need a mediator. I think you're overreacting."

"Overreacting?" he questioned. "You pulled a gun on Misty; she, in turn, drew a gun on you. You two definitely need a mediator, so one or both of you don't end up in the morgue."

Playfully punching Kyle in the arm, Kara laughed in spite of herself.

"Why do you care so much, mister? Are you worried about me?"

Kyle parked the car in the driveway. Cutting the engine, he turned toward Kara so she had his full attention. "Yes. I always worry about you. I worry that you get in over your head sometimes, I worry about whatever is haunting you. I worry about you taking a bath every night when you're tired. I'm always afraid you're going to fall asleep and drown. I worry about you from the time my eyes open in the morning, until they shut at night. I love you. How is it you don't know that by now?"

Kara reached out her hand to graze his face. "I know you love me, Kyle. But right now I cannot reciprocate those feelings. I am too much of a mess. It wouldn't be fair to you to enter into anything the way I am now. I wouldn't be able to give you the time and attention you need." She searched his eyes for understanding. "You understand, don't you?"

"Of course I understand," Kyle spoke softly. "I just wanted you to know that I am here for you. I've always been in your corner. You don't need guys like Jason who lack the intelligence to know a good woman when they have one and to walk away from that woman to wife an infatuation that will be over in a few months. He is a child, I am a man, and one day you will come to know the difference," Kyle informed her. "Come, let's grab your things so we can get in the house. From the look of those gray clouds forming, a storm is brewing."

A storm is brewing, but it has little to do with this weather and more with pure attraction. He has me turned on, but I will never tell. Kyle one. Me zero.

EIGHTEEN

I SHOULD HAVE TAKEN HER LAST BREATH BY NOW. Everything in me is screaming for me to be patient. All things have a place in time. Things must be completed in decency and order. A few more weeks' time is all she has left. Then she will be mine. The torturing that she has done to my spirit. She's undeserving of life, more so after running over that child and letting another take the fall. Spineless she was. She took a child's life, something I vowed I would never do, which is why she continues to walk the earth. Now I am filled with regret. If I had gotten rid of her long ago, that unfortunate child would not have suffered the fate they did that night. I blame myself. But time still ticks and the clock continues to wind down. It's only a matter of time.

NINETEEN

"EXCUSE ME."

"Yes, dear, how may I help you?" Kara smiled at the elderly gray-haired lady with her glasses hanging around her neck. She looked exactly as a librarian should look, the friendly type you pictured in children's books, that probably had milk and cookies sitting out on her table for the neighborhood kids to have when they ran off the bus from school.

"Hi." Kara smiled. "I was wondering where to go if I want to look up a newspaper from 1997."

"Of course, dear. Let me walk you over to that area."

"Thank you." Kara followed as the librarian whose nametag read Mary guided her to the Newsroom.

"Everything is digital now, you know." Mary pointed to an old computer placed on a six-foot table, indicating for Kara to sit in the chair in front of the computer. Entering her login information, the computer whirred to life. "There you are, dear. Just click here for newspaper clippings and type in the search title of what you are hoping to find."

"You've been a great help. Thank you," Kara said as she placed her purse on the table and typed in "1997 obituary, Charles Lee Anthony, Washington, DC." In two seconds an image of Kara's father appeared on the computer screen.

Hi, Daddy. Scrolling down the search engine results, Kara found what she was looking for: her father's obituary.

Washington Post
>Sunday, May 31, 1997
>On Wednesday, May 21, 1997. Charles Lee Anthony departed this earth. Beloved husband of the former Barbara Ann Jones; devoted father of Jaxson Lee Anthony; and Kellie Lee Anthony (deceased). He is also survived by a host of other relatives and friends. Mr. Anthony will be laid to rest at Lincoln Memorial Cemetery. The family would like to thank everyone during this difficult time and asks for your prayers to guide them through.

What is going on here? There is no mention of my mother or me anywhere. He was married to someone else?

Kara opened a new tab on the browser so she could search Google. She typed in the name Barbara Ann Jones and her father's name, praying she was wrong. She closed her eyes in disbelief as a photo of her therapist appeared on the screen. *Someone is plotting for me to go crazy. They must be. God, are you mad at me?* Kara was floored. Grabbing her purse from the table, she practically sprinted from the library.

"You have some explaining to do," Kara yelled. She'd arrived at her mother's Georgetown townhome in record time.

"Excuse me, you will not speak to your mother in that tone."

"Mother, stop it!" Gone was Kara's attitude of empathy about her mother's feelings. "I don't care how you feel. So

100

get over that. You will tell me the truth this day. I am not leaving here until you do." Kara put her foot down. Enough was enough already. She needed her mother to understand that she meant business. She was so angry she almost fell over Lucifer, her mother's dog, when she barged in.

"What is it that has you so tightly wound up?"

"Daddy was married to another woman?" Kara waited for her mother's reaction.

"Why would you say such a thing?"

"Mother, I've already asked you to stop it. Please stop. There is no more time for playing." Kara sat on the stool at the bar in her mother's Victorian-style kitchen, crossing her arms across her chest waiting for answers.

"Yes. He was married, okay?"

Well wonders will never cease—my mom finally tells the truth. "You and Daddy were having an affair?"

"No way. Your father was my husband. He was. He just had her too."

Kara stared at her delusional mother and wondered if she could hear the words she was speaking.

"No, Mom, he was her husband, he just had *you* too," Kara corrected her. "Why did you lie to me for all these years? It would have been okay if you and Daddy weren't married. It doesn't change the fact that he's my father." Kara eyed her, afraid of what she might say. "He is my father, isn't he?"

"How can you ask something like that? Of course he is your father." Kara's mother was offended.

Kara let out a sigh of relief. She hadn't been aware that

she was holding her breath. *At least that's true.*

"This is insane. Two of the most important people in my life have been lying to me for years. I'm sure you knew my therapist was Daddy's wife. Why did you choose her?"

"Because, it was the right thing to do. I owed her. We're even now."

Kara was beside herself trying to understand how one can be even after having another family with one's husband. But in her mother's mind that somehow made sense.

I must be in the twilight zone. This is not real. I must be dreaming, that's what it is. I'm dreaming.

"You were Daddy's mistress," she whispered. "This is all too much so close to the anniversary of his death. No wonder you never want to talk about him. This is a lot for me to take in. I can only imagine living it. But it all makes sense now, why he was never home."

"No, your father was never home because he was in the military. That is the truth."

"It's your truth. But I've just discovered that your truth has variations and I can't trust you. I'll get my information elsewhere."

Kara grabbed her bag, stomping to the door. She'd had enough of her lying mother for one day.

"I TRUSTED YOU!" Kara stormed into Dr. Jones's office interrupting a session she was in the process of having, screaming at the top of her lungs.

"Ms. Jones, I'm so sorry. She just barged her way in. I

couldn't stop her," the young receptionist said in a state of panic as she ran in the room behind an irate Kara. "Should I call security?"

"It's alright. Go on back to the front, Jeanine. I'll handle it from here." Barbara always as calm as a cucumber, turned to her client. "I'm sorry, Davis. Do you mind if we pick up next week? As you can see we're having a small emergency situation."

"Sure, next week same time."

"Absolutely. Don't forget what we discussed."

"I won't, Dr. Jones." He gave Kara a look of annoyance as he left the room, shutting the heavy oak door behind him.

"Kara, to what do I owe the honor of an unscheduled visit?"

"You lied to my face. I trusted you," Kara repeated. "How could you do this to me?"

"Please have a seat." Barbara motioned to the chaise.

"I'll stand."

"What did I do exactly?" Barbara inquired. "Because lying isn't one of them." She was patient with Kara. She understood her torment was real, the five-year-old girl in her trying to figure things out.

"You never told me that you are my father's wife," Kara accused.

"Why would *I* tell you that?" Barbara sat back in her chair getting comfortable anticipating that this would be a long session.

"Why wouldn't you tell me? I came to you for years

wondering about my father because my mother won't talk about him, and you knew. You knew all about him."

"I wanted to tell you, but, Kara, it wasn't my place to do so. What have I been telling you all this time? 'Do your research; there are other sources besides your mother to find the answers you seek.'" Barbara smiled softly. "You must have taken my advice because here you are. I know your mother didn't tell you. She's not built that way."

"You know my mother?"

"Victoria and I met briefly in the past, before Charles's untimely death."

"I always thought she chose you as my therapist when I was a teenager because of your religious beliefs, but she had other reasons."

"I'm not sure her reasons, but I was happy to get to know you, see what my daughter may have been like if she were here."

"My mother said she owed you."

Barbara cleared her throat. "If that's how she feels. But she doesn't owe me anything. It takes two to tango, and she didn't tango alone; otherwise you wouldn't be here."

"How can you be so nonchalant about this? I feel as if my world has shattered." Kara wanted to cry, but chose to display strength. She would save her tears for when she was alone.

"I've had a long time to come to terms with everything. I forgave Charles and your mother long ago. I choose to be happy. Holding on to toxic thoughts and what-ifs isn't good for anyone."

"My mother is nothing like you. She can't even process this. In her mind she and Daddy were just as much married as you and him."

"I suppose in a way they were. We had him to ourselves about the same amount of time. He produced two babies in each situation. Our families are a mirror image of each other's."

"Two babies?" Kara echoed. "I'm an only child."

Barbara closed her eyes disgusted with herself. *How did I let that slip?*

"Kara, maybe we should end for today. I've already said too much. You should speak more in-depth with your mother," Barbara said as she left Kara sitting in her office so she could get a breath of fresh air. Talking about events she had long ago buried was more than she had bargained for on this sunny afternoon, and she needed time to get her thoughts together before she and Kara sat down again. She was about to do something she'd sworn she would never do again as long as she lived. *I need to pay Victoria a visit.*

TWENTY

"I KNOW WHAT THIS IS. THIS IS DENIAL. BECAUSE I CANNOT believe my mother and my therapist have been lying to me since forever. Isn't there some code Dr. Jones is breaking? She shouldn't be allowed to be my therapist, right?"

"I do believe that is a conflict of interest. I'm sure you can file a complaint or sue if you want to."

Kara rested her head on the back of the sofa, closing her eyes, feeling the beginning of a headache determined to root itself.

"No, I don't want to sue her. As messed up as it is, she has helped me throughout the years and she says I feel like the daughter she lost. I don't want to take that from her." Kara curled her bare feet under her on the sofa and opened sad eyes to gaze at Kyle. "What did I do to be given this life? You think I was a mean person in my past life?"

"You could never be mean. That's not the type of person you are. This life or otherwise." Kyle sat at the other end of the couch, not feeling sorry for Kara because she was too strong of a woman and would resent him for that, but feeling love for her. He didn't know why her life was an eruptive volcano and sitting in the toilet at that moment. All he could try to do was be a good friend and partner to see her through this.

"None of this makes any sense. My mother said she owes Dr. Jones. Do you think it's because my dad began a family with her?"

"I'm pretty sure that has something to do with it. She

probably feels guilty and her way of making peace was to let Dr. Jones have a piece of you."

"The two of them both seem mentally unstable. I for one would not want to be a therapist to my husband's mistress's bastard child. And my mother should not have allowed her husband's wife to be my therapist. What kind of world am I living in?"

"When you say it out loud, it does sound pretty bad. The two of them don't come off as unstable to me, they just are both incredibly selfish. It looks as if neither of them thought about your best interest in this situation. In a way, it honestly seems as if they have an unhealthy attachment to one another and you are the pawn in their twisted game of keeping tabs on each other."

"A pawn." Kara pondered Kyle's statement. "That's exactly what I am." Her voice became animated. "Think about it. Someone is playing a game of cat and mouse with me by following me, leaving flowers with notes, forcing me into accidents; watching me." She stared at Kyle in bewilderment. "How could I have not known this? Don't you see, Kyle?"

"Not exactly," he responded slowly, trying to see where Kara was going. "I know that you do have someone trying to intimidate you, but I don't think it is a game at all. I believe your mother and your therapist are playing some sick game with one another. Even with you as a pawn, you aren't a part of that game. What we have going on with you is a very real situation, and I'm concerned about your safety."

"I know you are. I'm concerned about my safety as well. But I cannot stay here with you forever. Eventually I am going to have to face the demon that is out to get me."

"Don't worry, Kay A. We will find them. I guarantee you that," Kyle told her. "Now how about we do something else to take your mind off of all this. Will you allow me to take you to dinner?"

"I'm not really hungry." Kara gazed up at him apologetically. "I'll take a raincheck on dinner, but you know what you can help me do?"

Kyle cut his eyes at Kara unsure of what she was about to ask of him.

"What might that be?" he questioned.

"You can come with me down to District Seven so I can comb through their file room."

Kyle leaned on the door frame and crossed his arms. "Right now?"

"Yes, right now. Come on."

~ ~ ~

"Hi, Detective, how may I help you?"

"Hello. We're here to view a few records."

"Sure, no problem. You know where the record room is?"

"Yes, we'll be fine."

"Thank you so much for being here, Kyle." Kara smiled, grateful that Kyle had accompanied her to District Seven. Without a badge in possession, she wasn't sure how things would go.

"You know it's not a problem. What is it that we are looking for?"

"I want to see if they have a file on me."

"Why would there be a file on you?"

"Because I testified at Ryan's trial and my testimony isn't a part of his file."

"You think someone may have tampered with the file?"

"That's the only logical conclusion I could come to."

"Well, it should be easy to see who handled the file."

"Not really," Kara stated. "They could have walked in just like we did without logging our information and gone through the file taking what they needed with no one being the wiser."

"I hear you, but only a few people have the credentials to gain access back here."

"You do realize that a few people is the whole department and other departments? Anyone can get access back here if they want to," she pointed out.

"You're absolutely right. Not sure what I was thinking."

"This is such a misfortune that we can't find anything. Anyone could have my information by now."

TWENTY-ONE

"HELLO, VICTORIA."

"Why are you here?" Victoria was less than enthused about coming face-to-face with Barbara; her nemesis, a blast from the past she'd tried to forget existed. "I thought we agreed long ago never to see or speak to one another ever again."

"That's what I thought as well." Barbara was in agreement. "Things change, however. May I come in?"

"No, you may not." Victoria was adamant that Barbara would not cross her threshold for one second as long as there was breath in her lungs. She couldn't believe the nerve of Charles's widower. "Whatever it is that you have to say can be said from your perch on that step or not at all."

"Victoria." Barbara was indignant. "I will not continue to stand on this step as if I am a peasant begging for food."

Victoria held her ground, staring at her unwelcome visitor, not uttering a word, indifferent to how she felt.

"How about you join me on an afternoon stroll?" Barbara relented. "I'm sure my being here is a shock, and I owe you an apology for stopping by unannounced, but I really do need to speak with you about an urgent matter." Barbara gazed into hauntingly sad eyes. "Please, Victoria, please. It's important," she pled softly.

"Fine," came the reluctant reply. "I'll give you ten minutes of my time and then I have to move on."

"Thank you. That's all I ask."

"Kara came to see me today with news that she's discovered the truth about her past. Our past."

"Is that all?" Victoria waved her hands across her face. "I already know. Is that what you rushed yourself over here to tell me? I'm sure you could have mailed me a letter with that information."

"What you don't know," Barbara continued, ignoring the pointed jabs Victoria was determined to make at her, "is that I accidentally let it slip that you had another child."

"You what?" Victoria stopped in her tracks, her tone menacing. Barbara halted as well.

"Victoria, it was a complete accident. I was lost in a mom—" Barbara's words were cut short by the resounding smack Victoria placed across her mouth. Barbara's purse fell to the ground in her startled state.

"You have some nerve telling her that news. What is wrong with you?"

Barbara stood up and lunged at Victoria on the sidewalk, tussling until they both fell in a heap on the ground. Barbara got the advantage and sat on Victoria's chest to keep her from moving.

"Are you crazy? You don't walk around slapping people in the face because they say something you don't like. This is probably the reason Charles never fully left me to be with you. You're a loose cannon."

"You watch your mouth. Nothing you and Charles had can ever compare to what he and I had."

"You're right. I don't know what it feels like to be a mistress waiting for a man to leave his family and when he doesn't you create your own family with him anyway."

"Charles left his family long before I ever entered the picture," Victoria enlightened her. "Because if he didn't, there would be no me."

Barbara slowly stood up allowing Victoria to rise from the sidewalk. She eyed her as she brushed herself off, waving at the curious bystanders that were watching their altercation with interest. "It doesn't matter, Victoria. I'm too old; and so are you, to worry about the things that Charles was doing and why. My sole purpose for this meeting is purely informative. Kara knows there was another baby, and I want to give you the heads-up so you have ample time to figure out what it is you're going to tell her."

"Typical Annie girl. Always leaving me to clean up your messes."

"What exactly are you implying?"

"Don't play coy with me. You know exactly what I'm talking about."

"Please elaborate." Barbara had had enough of Victoria's high and mighty attitude. If anyone was wronged during all the time they had known one another, it was definitely her.

"Your daughter."

Barbara's face turned beet red. "Don't you mention my daughter; you have no right," she replied angrily. "You're the reason she's not here."

"What! I'm the one who helped you bury the body. Let us not forget."

"I am well aware of that fact. No need to remind me. However, it doesn't change the fact that you took her away from me."

"Your daughter was an accident. You really need to get over that. It's been twenty-five years."

"Oh, I have to get over it?"

Victoria stared Barbara directly in her eyes. "Yes, you do. You knew back then that it was a mistake. You lost one, I lost one. I feel like we're even."

"We're nowhere near even. I'm sorry I came here to warn you. I should have known you hadn't changed. Some part of me is continually searching for a different outcome of this life we have lived, but I'm beginning to see there is only one outcome. I'm sorry that you are the one that received the opportunity to be Kara's mother. You don't deserve her. It's a wonder she turned out the way she did with you as a mother."

"How dare you insult me out here in the street, in my neighborhood."

"You never stick to the issues. Who cares about this neighborhood? You hit me in the street, and that was an okay thing to do, but not this? What I'm saying to you is far more important than the demographics of where we are. You are a horrible person and mother. But for whatever reason God saw it fit for you to raise Kara and allow me to be a surrogate of sorts."

"Not God. ME!" Victoria was beside herself in anger, needing to emphasize her control over Barbara. "I saw fit. I felt horrible for the things that happened to you, and against my better judgment and because of a weakness at that time, I allowed the interaction. I gave you that, among other things you didn't know what to do with. Don't you ever forget it."

"I don't need this. Your daughter is angry at both of us. I have done all I can do here. I never want to see you again. There is no reason for us to speak further."

"There was no reason for us to speak in the first place," Victoria shouted behind a retreating Barbara, angry that once again she'd allowed Chuck's wife to get the best of her.

"Who are you?"

"No, my dear, the question is not who I am, but who are you?" I curiously regarded the well put together woman that had sashayed her way into my home as if she were fresh out of a Diane von Fürstenberg ad with a little girl I assumed was her daughter in tow. There was an air about her that commanded respect.

"Victoria Anthony," I told her, completely unfazed, knowing that I could handle myself if the need arose. "How may I help you?"

Barbara took in the young woman's appearance: barefoot; coral, long flowy dress; and a sunhat. She hated to admit that she was pretty in an unconventional way. Fair skinned with violet eyes a little too large for her face, covered by long curled lashes, freckles sprinkled across her nose; there was a freshness about her. She looked fun. As painful as it was to have to admit to herself, Barbara could see the attraction. A complete opposite of herself.

"I have these to give to you."

Taking the package from the woman, Victoria was glowing. Having just entered her second trimester of her second pregnancy, nothing could dampen her day. Not even this wayward stranger determined to rain on her sunshine with her negativity.

"For me?"

"Yes, a gift from Charles and I?"

"Charles?" A nervous shudder went through Victoria. It wasn't the fact that this woman was bringing her a gift from Charles, it was the how she said "Charles and I" with ownership.

"I'm sorry. I didn't get your name."

"Barbara. Barbara Anthony."

"Oh. Are you kin to Charles? I'm sorry I look such a fright. Won't you have a seat? I can't believe that he didn't announce someone from his family would be stopping by today. Military mail being what it is, his letter must be caught up in the mail."

"Please open the package," Barbara spoke softly.

Untying the rope that held the package covered in brown paper together, Victoria's eyes began to cloud as disbelief overcame her.

"Chuck," Victoria whispered with her eyes glued to the photos. "What is this?" came the accusing tone.

"My family. See, that first photo is my husband Charles and I on our wedding day. The second photo is our two children."

"Mommy!" Both women looked back toward the family room as a tiny toddler ran in the room.

"Cupcake, go get your doll and then wait for me in the kitchen, okay?"

The adorable tot smiled. "Okay, Mommy."

"Cute kid."

"Thank you. Chuck and I did well with that one. We are hoping the same for this one." She touched her belly softly.

Barbara's heart sank. "That's my husband Charles's daughter? And you're pregnant now?"

"So it seems. My, my, we have quite the dilemma, don't we?"

"Yes, yes we do," Barbara told the woman as she and her daughter entered the home and she shut the door behind her.

TWENTY-TWO

WALTZING INTO THE ROOM BYPASSING THE FAMILIAR CHAISE
on the wall, Kara stood in front of Dr. Jones with a frown
on her face and an attitude in her walk.

"Why the negative energy today, Kara?"

"You know why." Kara wasn't in the mood for her
calm-spirited therapist today. She was spoiling for a fight.

"I think it's in our best interest to end this relationship,"
she stated bluntly. "Due to the presiding circumstances, I
feel as if it is a conflict of interest. But more importantly, I
no longer trust you."

"That is a reasonable request; however, it is not
necessary."

"It's very necessary. Your betrayal cuts deep, deeper
than the others because I've known you for years. You
have always been my ally, my sounding board when my
mother and I were at odds. To find out that my mother was
your husband's mistress is incredibly creepy to me and
deceitful on both of your ends. How the two of you can
keep a secret for so long is mind-boggling."

"I understand your resentment, your anger, but you can
take this opportunity to ask me questions about your father;
about me."

"Why now? Why not share this information with me
before? I would have trusted you much more. I would have
been able to understand. You both left me to be ambushed."

"It wasn't my place to tell you about that relationship. I
am not your mother."

"Yet in some ways you are more my mother than my own mother could ever be."

"While that may be, your mother and I suffered from our own issues, and as hard to believe as it may be, I have always respected the fact that she is your mother and what she says goes."

"Well, I'm glad you feel that way. Nevertheless, you and I are completely done. There is no way you can counsel me, and you have so many of your own issues."

"That's what makes me great at my job; I can sympathize because of my issues."

"I knew I could find you here." Both women turned toward the door as a disheveled Jason entered Dr. Jones's office.

A dull ache forming behind her left eye, Kara took it upon herself to have a seat on the chaise. *What now?*

"Excuse me, may I ask you to identify yourself?" Dr. Jones asked.

Piercing eyes focused on Kara.

"I'm Jason. Kara's ex-fiancée."

"Oh, so you're the elusive Jason."

"You've been talking about me?" His eyes were still trained on Kara.

Averting her eyes from his, Kara shrugged. "Why are you stalking me?"

"Because you won't take my calls. I'm tired of this avoidance dance you're playing with me."

"There is no game. I am not playing with you. I want you to leave me alone. You would think that you'd get the

118

hint by now." Kara jumped up, marching toward Jason. *So much for trying to stay calm and indifferent.*

"You left me. You and Misty are completely delusional expecting me to be understanding of this situation." She was in his face now, pointing her finger into his chest. "Why will you both not go away and leave me be? Let me live my life like I allow you to live yours."

"Because I miss you. I made a mistake, and now I feel stuck in my situation. I want you back."

What? His reluctant admission caught Kara by surprise. "Oh, I get it, this is some type of cruel joke that is being played on me, right? Let me guess, Misty is in the hall recording this entire conversation. Tell her come in too. Let's stop this charade."

"Kara, what is wrong with you? Misty is not in the hallway; it's just me."

"Well excuse me if I happen to think that this is some sort of comedy show. What do you want, Jason? I don't have the energy to fight with you." *I'm at odds with everyone. God, where are you? Help me.*

"To talk."

"Well talk." Kara was happy to have Dr. Jones as a third party in case Jason or she ended up completely losing it.

"I want to start by apologizing for Misty approaching you that day at the office resulting in you pulling a gun on her and her being suspended. I know how much your job means to you. I'll tell her to drop the complaint against you. It's obvious she began the conversation to provoke you, and in all fairness anyone would have lost their cool if dealing with the same circumstances."

Kara remained silent letting him continue.

"I also want to apologize for my behavior. It was out of character for me and completely unfair to you. I owed you much more than the way I behaved. When you know better, you do better. I'm here hoping to show you the better."

"Those are pretty words, Jason, but I'm still confused as to what it is you are seeking from me."

"A second chance."

"No." Kara's tone was final. "I don't trust you and I never will. You and Misty can have one another."

"You're trying to leave me?" The three occupants in the office turned in surprise as the door opened hard banging against the wall, with Misty barging her way in.

Kara closed her eyes willing the floor to swallow her whole, mentally kicking herself because she had left her weapon at home because she was temporarily unable to carry a firearm legally.

"Jason, is that true?"

"Baby, what are you doing here?" Jason resembled a wide-eyed doe caught in headlights.

"Following you. What does it look like? What are you doing here?"

"I needed to see Kara. I knew I could find her here."

"See her for what? I heard something about a second chance, so I repeat, are you trying to leave me?" Misty was getting angrier and angrier by the second.

"How about we all sit down to discuss this?"

"Who are you?" Misty demanded.

"Dr. Jones. Kara's therapist."

"Nice to finally meet you, Doctor. I've heard so much about you from Kara, who can't seem to get her life together ever," Misty stated. "You may want to mind your business. We all don't need to discuss anything. This is between me and my husband."

"With all due respect, you're in my office, so let's handle this like adults," Barbara pushed.

Kara was annoyed they'd been sitting in this Girl Scouts kumbaya circle for over an hour and nothing with getting accomplished. Jason wanted out, Misty wanted him to stay, and Kara was just very bored with the whole scenario.

This is my karma for Ryan. I just know it.

"I am not a mistake." Misty pouted.

"I was infatuated with you because you were fun, something my relationship with Kara was missing at the time. I'm not proud of my actions. Now I'm dealing with my family being upset. No one likes you. You know it."

"So this change of behavior is all because your mother doesn't like me?"

"Excuse me, I hate to interrupt this marriage counseling session on my dime, but since I am unmarried, I really don't need to be here for this. I have no interest in listening to other people's marital problems."

Misty pulled out her gun. "You will sit and listen."

Kara kept her eyes trained on Misty's weapon as she

heard Dr. Jones on the phone with 911.

"I know I pulled a weapon on you at the office, Misty, but you and I both know I wasn't going to pull the trigger that day no matter how much you provoked me. Put your weapon away. I'm suspended, so we're even."

"We're nowhere near even," Misty stated, standing up and walking closer to Kara.

Kara waited until Misty was directly in front of her and rambling before she reached out knocking the weapon from Misty's hands. She then placed her in a chokehold. "Let that be the last time you pull a weapon on me," Kara whispered in Misty's ear, holding her down until the police arrived.

After giving her statement to the police, Kara hightailed it out of Barbara's office. Today had been a little over the top for her. What she couldn't forget was how Jason had just sat there. *How did I never realize how weak he is? Thank you, God, you truly do work in mysterious ways.*

TWENTY-THREE

"DRINK UP."

"Are you intentionally trying to get me drunk? I've lost count of the shots you've bought me."

Kyle winked at Kara. "Now why would I try and do something like that? You have to learn to live a little."

The bartender gazed at Kara in sympathy when she looked over to him for help. Shaking his head with a slight grin on his face, he proceeded with wiping the bar down.

"I'll be right back," Kyle yelled over the loud music. "Nature calls."

"Okay," she yelled back as the sounds of techno music drifted through the air.

After ending her emotionally exhausting and draining final session with Dr. Jones and the unwelcome Mr. and Mrs. McCarthy, Kara had gotten the urge for a much-needed drink. Having a gun pulled on you could do that, which is how she and Kyle had come to be occupying bar space at Policy on 14th Street in Northwest DC.

"Is that your boyfriend you're with?" The bartender that had regarded her with a smile earlier came over to ask her.

"Who, Kyle?" Kara laughed. "No. He's my partner. I'm a detective." Her tongue was a little looser than normal due to the alcohol.

"Is that right?"

"It is." Kara's inebriated spirit was merry and in agreement, enjoying the fact that his voice sounded like smooth caramel dripping over chocolate.

"Would you like some water to chase those shots you and your partner have been hitting pretty hard?"

"You must be a mind reader. I am in desperate need of water." She sighed a breath of relief. "You are my saving grace. Thank you, uh, uh." She paused realizing she didn't know his name.

"Aaron," he said as he placed a tall glass of water in front of her, garnished with lemon and lime slices. "You're welcome, gorgeous."

"Aaron. See, I knew you were a mind reader." Kara blushed, gratefully picking up the iced glass of water and gulping it down in seconds to hide her flushed cheeks. "I'm Kara," she introduced herself after every drop of water had successfully entered her body.

"Refill?" Aaron asked. Kara nodded gratefully.

"I know who you are," he stated while pouring her another glass of water. "You don't remember me, do you?"

Uh, uh, who is this guy? Kara's body was immediately on alert. Her sixth sense shifted into high gear as she felt herself quickly sobering up.

"Should I?"

He shrugged. "Maybe, maybe not. We used to be neighbors before your family moved away after your father passed away."

Kara squinted at him realizing he was indeed vaguely familiar as a memory flooded her consciousness.

"Mommy, can I go outside and ride my bike?"

"I don't know, cupcake. Can you?"

"May I go outside?" Kara instantly corrected her

124

mistake.

"Of course you may, beautiful."

"Yay. Now I can be outside when Daddy comes."

Victoria took the last batch of cookies out of the oven, setting them on a rack to cool.

"Come here, muffin. I need to talk to you for a minute," she told her five-year-old as she sat in a wooden chair and pulled her into her lap.

"Yes?"

"Your Daddy may not be coming home today. That's what he called to tell me."

Kara stuck her bottom lip out disappointed, trying to hold back tears. "Why?"

"Well, he said he would definitely be home tomorrow because he knows his little girl is missing him."

"Yay!" Kara was all grins again. "Mommy, don't be sad. Tomorrow will be here sooner than you think." She wrapped her small arms around her mother to console her before climbing off her lap.

"I'm not sad, cupcake. You make everything better. That Darby kid from next door is outside. You can ride your bike with him while he's out there."

"Yay!"

"Aaron Darby," Kara whispered. "I remember," she said, gazing up at the tall brown-skinned man in front of her.

"So, you do know me, huh? Helps to realize I'm not a stranger, right?" He winked at her.

"Yeah. You were outside when everything happened that day. It's all coming back to me now."

"Your mother had just called you into the house; I was standing there getting ready to put my bike away when your father pulled up. When he got out of the car, he had a white teddy bear in his hands."

"Oh my God." The tears began descending. After the meeting with Dr. Jones and too many drinks, Kara was proving the theory of emotions and alcohol not mixing well. "You're a living breathing witness. That day is all a blur to me."

"I can imagine. I didn't mean to make you cry." Aaron picked up a cocktail napkin and gently wiped the tears from her face. His fingers lingered a few seconds longer than they should have. Picking up another cocktail napkin he wrote his number down. "Let's talk later. Call me." He passed her the napkin.

"I would love that." Kara smiled shyly as she reached for the napkin, their fingers brushing each other's lightly. Feeling a jolt of electricity from his touch, she quickly placed the napkin in her purse.

He gave her a knowing smile. "I felt it too." His deep voice whispered as he leaned in and placed a soft kiss on her cheek. "I always wondered where you were and what you were up to."

"What's going on over here?" An angry, brash tone of voice shattered their moment.

Kara sat back relieving herself of Aaron's immediate body space, looking over at Kyle.

"Hey! We're just catching up with one another. It turns out that Aaron here is an old friend." She was desperately trying to de-escalate the tension that was now present in the air.

"Old friend, huh?" Kyle was not amused. "Oh yeah, so you let this *old friend* kiss you? You won't even allow kisses from me, and I've more than earned them. What did this idiot do?" Kyle's voice had escalated to a shout.

Kara lightly touched Kyle's arm. "Kyle, what in the world is wrong with you? I think you've had too much to drink," she stated, appalled to see Kyle behaving this way. This was a side of him she had never seen before. He always kept a laid-back demeanor. "We should go." She began standing up reaching into her purse to place bills on the countertop.

"No. I'll leave when I'm ready." Kyle removed his arm from her grip. "She's spoken for," he announced, leaning over the bar grabbing Aaron's collar in one fluid motion.

"Doesn't seem that way to me." Aaron smirked, as he pushed Kyle's hands off his shirt, letting go of the bottle and wiping rag he was holding to give drunken Kyle his full attention.

"Kyle, you stop this right now. I am not spoken for, and you will not fight Aaron. He has done nothing wrong. Come on, let's go." Kara was completely sobered up at this point. Kyle was acting like a madman, and she needed to get him out of here quickly before this situation went from bad to worse, because she knew without a doubt, a fight was brewing.

"Stop telling me what to do and be quiet."

"You should listen to her. It's clear you've had too much to drink. Go walk it off," Aaron told Kyle.

Kara was beside herself. Never in life had Kyle spoken to her in that tone of voice. Who was this person? Drunk or otherwise, he was never disrespectful.

"Kyle, let's go right now. Security is walking this way. Please let this go." She knew Kyle had his service pistol on him and they didn't need the extra conflict from that. "Please. Please, Kyle. Don't do this."

"Fine. Let's get out of here. He's not worth it anyway."

Kara was happy as they began making their way toward the door to leave. She'd had enough excitement for one evening.

Thank you, God. Now if you can please just send me peace.

TWENTY-FOUR

I SEE HER WITH THE TWO OF THEM. SHE SEEMS TO BE SMITTEN with the bartender. Too bad her partner came and ruined things for her. I cannot believe that these idiots are about to fight over a corpse. If they only knew what I did, they wouldn't waste their time and would find a way to enjoy the rest of their night. This woman isn't worth the trouble.

"You alright out here?"

"Yes, Officer. I didn't see you."

"Where you headed?"

"I was going to the bar, but I think I'll head on home now. I'm no longer in the mood to be sociable."

"Okay. Well you be careful out here."

"I will. Thank you, Officer."

"It's Detective Harris." He handed me his business card and tipped his hat. "Have a good night then."

"You too, Detective. Good night."

Pulling my hoodie down further, I casually walked past the bar determined to make myself scarce as the detective sat in his car behind me observing me.

I lost my head tonight. Focused so hard on my prey I let my guard down and allowed my face to be seen. This may present a problem. Later on. Plan B.

TWENTY-FIVE

"THANK YOU FOR MEETING ME HERE."

"Of course. Thank you for the invite."

Kara was happy Aaron had come to meet her at Ebenezer's Coffee House on F Street in Northeast, DC.

"I never knew they had people sing live here."

"I know. It's one of the reasons I really love coming here. The atmosphere is perfect. Very relaxing."

"I see," Aaron said as he sat down, lifting her hand to his lips to place a soft kiss.

Kara found herself blushing at such a blatant display of chivalry. She casually took a sip of her Frappuccino, trying to diffuse the electric intensity of having him touch her.

"It's nice to see you without the angry guy around." He gave her a knowing wink.

"Who, Kyle?" Kara laughed. "He's harmless. That night he just had a little too much to drink and wasn't being his normal funny self."

"That and he doesn't want you getting too close to me." Aaron grinned. "Which is very perceptive of him because I can guarantee you that my intentions are less than pure."

The fire Kara felt deep down in her loins was almost her undoing. She'd never felt an attraction this magnetic before. Not even with Ryan or Jason. She'd have to tread lightly in Aaron's presence and be careful not to become as giddy as a schoolgirl.

"Is that so?"

"Absolutely."

"Um, how is your sister? I vaguely remember her."

"She's good. She's a nurse over at George Washington Hospital."

"How nice. I was born there."

"Me too. Look at that, we have something in common."

"You are reaching." Kara's eyes were dancing in merriment. "But I do applaud your efforts."

"I figured you would." Aaron flashed an easy smile. "She's good, however. A nurse by night, mom by day."

"She's a mother? Good for her. How do you like being an uncle?"

"I love it. The three little monsters really keep me going."

"Wow, there's three of them?"

"Yup. Two boys and a girl. Ages five, three, and eight months. The girl is eight months and more of a handful than the boys already. She has Uncle Aaron wrapped around her little fingers, I must admit." His face was beaming with joy.

"I bet she does." Kara laughed as he promptly pulled photos out of his well-used leather wallet. "Proud Uncle, I see."

"Very. I couldn't be more proud. I'd do anything for these little ones of mine. Uncle Aaron is always to the rescue."

"I know you would. How does your sister manage it all? I can barely take care of myself some days. I couldn't imagine dividing my time equally between three kids."

"Her husband, Neil, is pretty hands on. I'm one of his

biggest fans. He makes sure he has everything under control at home so Deidre can do the job she loves without worrying about home life. The two of them are an awesome team." Aaron looked deeply into Kara's eyes. "I hope to have what they do someday."

"You will. The great guys always do."

"You think I'm a great guy, huh?" He gave her a knowing smile.

"I was just saying." Her voice trailed off.

"Saying that you like and adore me? It's not a secret. I had already gathered as much."

"You are silly."

"A definite oversight. So tell me about yourself."

After regaling him of the recent events in her life, Kara was sure she'd run him off with all of her drama. She was not even sure why she had shared so much information. Something about him made him trustworthy to her. And she was impressed that he wasn't running for the hills.

"That's pretty intense. You seem to be handling it very well."

"Well three days ago when I landed in your bar, I was at my wits' end."

"I can't tell you how radiant you looked that day; a little inebriated, but radiant nevertheless."

"Gee, thank you. I think."

"Definitely a compliment. Do you think your mother went back to George Washington Hospital when she was pregnant with your brother? If so, my sister may be able to pull her old records. It's worth a shot to try at least."

Kara smiled. "You would do that for me? Why?"

"Because, as quiet as it's kept, you just may be the girl turned woman of my dreams. And that woman I would do anything for."

"There is no way you are harboring a crush from when we were tiny tots running around the yard."

Aaron shrugged. "Stranger things have happened. I'm a firm believer you can meet your soul mate at the edge of three."

"You're right about that, stranger things have happened. You've made me a believer." Kara nodded in agreement. "If you can find out any type of information without your sister getting into any disciplinary trouble, that would be amazing."

Aaron pulled out his cell phone. "Sorry to wake you, Dee. How are the kids? Napping? That's good. Quick question, can you look up medical records for Victoria Anthony? I will text you her birthdate and address later on. Thanks, babe, you're the best big sister in the world. Too much, a little much, okay. I still think you're the best. Love you too. Bye."

Kara sat quietly enjoying their easy sibling banter, somewhat jealous of a life she never was able to have with any of her siblings.

Aaron winked at Kara. "Done. She'll let us know what she finds by tonight."

"You are the absolute greatest. Thank you so much for helping me."

"You don't have to thank me. It is my pleasure to help

out an old friend." His smile widened. "Potential new friend."

"You're persistent, I'll give you that."

"Without persistence, how does one accomplish anything?"

"How do they indeed?"

"Say, let's get out of here and take a stroll to the Smithsonian."

"Really?" *Oh, how I love the museum. Maybe he is a soul mate.*

"Really. How about it?" He dropped a few bills on the table to handle the check, but held his hand out for her to take.

"You think I'll follow you anywhere don't you?" she asked, placing her hand into his.

"Here's hoping," he said as his hand tightly closed around hers and they exited the coffee shop together.

TWENTY-SIX

"THIS IS A NICE SURPRISE." KARA SMILED INTO THE PHONE.

"Is that so?"

"Absolutely so."

"Good. Are you free today?"

Kara thought about what was on her agenda besides trying to deal with her difficult mother. "Depends on what you have planned."

"Who said I have anything planned? I could just be wondering about your day," he quipped.

"Based off the context clues, I'm betting there is more to that." Kara laughed. She closed her eyes in delight as Aaron's deep laughter serenaded her ears.

"Okay, you caught me. I would like to take you out today, but only if you have time."

"I do believe that can be arranged, Mr. Darby."

"One of my favorite statements from you."

"Believe me, you'll come to love many more."

"I have every intention of doing just that."

Kara blushed at his seductive tone. "I have absolutely no doubt in your abilities."

"I'm loving the extra vote of confidence. Where shall I pick you up?"

"I can come to you." Kara had no intention of showing Aaron her unique living arrangements at the moment.

"You're going to deny me the opportunity of being a gentleman by escorting you to the car and holding your door open?"

"You'll find other ways to impress me, I'm sure."

"Touché, mon cheri, touché."

Kara's cell vibrated in her hand. She moved the phone away from her ear to see that Aaron had texted her an address.

"You sure move quickly." Kara laughed into the phone. "I received your text."

"Quick in some regards, slowly in others."

Her breath caught with the end of his statement, as her face heated up while she anticipated what a night of lovemaking would be like with him.

"Touché. What time should I meet you at this address?"

"How soon can you be ready?"

"In a breeze." Kara laughed.

Aaron chuckled. "How many minutes are there in a breeze exactly? Ballpark it for me."

"Twenty minutes tops. I can be ready to be at this address that you sent me and do whatever it is you have planned for me."

"Are you flirting with me?"

"Always," Kara said, surprising herself with her own boldness. Something about Aaron brought this playful, flirtatious side out of her.

"Good, I like it and appreciate your honesty."

"Let me get off this phone so I can get ready."

"Perfect. I'm looking forward to seeing you soon."

"Likewise, mister, likewise."

As Kara drove to the location Aaron had sent her, she

realized he had gone through quite a lot when she pulled up to the Smithsonian to find him standing out front with a bouquet of violet roses. Kara rolled the car window down as he approached the car with a man following close behind him.

"Kara, we're glad you could join us. Raoul here is going to take your car and valet it for you."

"Very nice, Mr. Darby, very nice," Kara acknowledged appreciatively as she exited the vehicle relinquishing her car to Raoul.

"May I?" Aaron extended his elbow for her to take.

Kara failed to hold back her smile. "Yes, you may," she told him as she took hold of his arm. "This is amazing," she whispered as they entered the ominous building.

"How did you manage this?" Kara was interested to know how Aaron had the power to get them into the Smithsonian after hours.

"A gentleman never alludes to his secrets." He smiled brilliant white teeth down at her as they strolled toward the area he was seeking.

Kara was amazed. There in the middle of the lobby, a grand piano had been brought in, accompanied by a pianist and a full band. A candlelit dinner table for two awaited them. Leading Kara to her chair, Aaron held it out as she sat. Placing the bouquet in the empty vase on the table as their centerpiece, he then sat down to join her.

"This is—" Kara shook her head in bewilderment "—I don't know what to call it. Just nothing short of amazing." She smiled into Aaron's eyes as the musicians began to play softly. "This is amazing."

Aaron winked at her. "You ain't seen nothing yet."

Merriment sparkled in Kara's eyes. The night had only just begun, and already she was having more fun with Aaron than she could recall having in a long time.

"Thank you."

"You're welcome, though I haven't done anything."

"I just want to thank you for being so nice to me and appearing normal."

"Not *being* normal, huh?" He laughed. "Just *appearing* that way."

Kara gazed into his magnetic eyes. "Seriously, you have no idea how much I needed a peaceful night like this one. My life has been so chaotic lately. This is an amazing reprieve from all of that."

"I'm glad to be able to help in any capacity I can."

Kara continued staring into Anthony's eyes thinking about how they had been as children, back when he used to call her Kary.

"Kary, you can do it."

"No I can't. I need my Daddy."

"Your dad's not here. Come on. I'll protect you."

"You promise?"

"I promise. I won't let you fall."

"Okay. I am trusting you."

"You can always trust me. Now peddle."

"Okay."

This handsome man taught me how to ride a bicycle, one four-year-old helping out another.

"You taught me how to ride a bike. Do you remember that?"

"Oh, you mean when all you had to do was peddle?" He chuckled. "Of course I remember that. You were this whiny little annoying kid that my mom made me play with."

Kara's mouth dropped open with feigned shocked indignation. "I was not whiny," she protested.

"It's okay." Aaron laughed as he reached for her hand from across the table. "You grew out of it."

Kara laughed with him. "Well geez, thanks, I guess."

"Come on, go ahead and admit it to yourself. You were whiny."

She squinted her eyes at him. "Okay, well maybe a little."

"Now, see, don't you feel better? Honesty can truly set you free."

"Well I guess when it's worded like that, it can be freeing."

Aaron bestowed a sexy smile on her as a reward for her honesty. "How is your mother?" he asked Kara as their dinner was served.

"A tragic disaster."

His eyes widened in response to her statement, yet he remained silent allowing her to continue.

"I mean, she just has no regard for how her actions affect me. She's beyond the selfish mark."

"What seems to be the issue?"

"Oh, Aaron," Kara sighed, "what isn't the issue? I don't

even know where to begin the ultimate tale of tales with that one."

"We have all night." His statement was more of a suggestion.

"Do we now?"

"As much time as you allow."

"I do believe my calendar is currently free, but let's talk about you instead. How is your family?"

"I know a deterrent when I see one, but I'll allow it this one time." He smiled. Kara enjoyed watching the side of his lips crinkle with his smile. "My parents both passed away a few years back. My ex-wife and I share joint custody of our daughter, Carrie, and they live in California."

"An ex-wife and a daughter, huh?"

"Yeah, the woman I wanted got away, so I had to settle for a runner-up, and we see how that ended up."

"How old is your daughter?"

"Four."

"Good age."

"I think so too. She's a lot of fun. I can't wait for you to be able to meet her."

"Oh really? You don't think it's too soon for me to meet your daughter?"

"Really. You two will get along great. You'll meet soon enough. Definitely not tomorrow, but soon."

"You're very sure of yourself, I see."

"Is there any other way to be?"

Kara laughed at his blatant cockiness. "No, no, I guess not."

TWENTY-SEVEN

NOW SHE PROBABLY THINKS SHE'S FANCY. HAS THIS MAN wining and dining her at the Smithsonian after dark. I hope this doesn't give her a false sense of security. There is nowhere on this magnificent green earth that God created where I wouldn't be able to find her and get a hold of her. It matters not who is around her and who she thinks can protect her. I am always near, and she is never very far from my grasp. Never.

TWENTY-EIGHT

"SO, WHAT'S THE STORY, MOM? YOU HONESTLY HAVE NO intention of ever speaking with me to rectify the situation, I gather?" Kara was beside herself with anger because her mother was being her normal self, acting like everything was normal and they didn't have this huge elephant in the room.

"If the topic is your father then the answer is no. You know how I feel about the subject, case closed."

"Okay, but what about this?" Kara slapped a baby sonogram on the table.

Victoria's eyes widened in shock.

"Where did you get that?"

Tears raced down Kara's face. "Mother, it doesn't matter where it came from; it's yours. So please tell me what happened to my baby brother." Aaron's sister Deidre had been able to find a partial record for Kara's mother, and it turned out the baby had been born alive.

"I don't have to discuss this with you." Victoria stood to leave the room.

"Oh no, Mother, you are not going anywhere." Kara gently nudged her mother back into her chair. "Yes, you do have to discuss it, and that's exactly what we're going to do. Right now." Kara crossed her arms. "You tell me the truth this instant. You cannot keep up this charade forever. Come clean already. What is wrong with you? I'm your daughter. I will love you no matter what it is. I'm just curious about a childhood I know so little about and a brother I never knew existed."

"Kara, do not confuse our roles. I am the mother; you are the child."

"That may be so, Mother, but you're the one acting as if you are a child at the moment. Stop finding ways to stall this conversation. Where is my brother? You are going to have to answer that question eventually, one way or another. What did you do?" Kara's voice was accusory.

"I will not be interrogated in my own home. I am not one of your detainees."

Taking a deep breath in frustration, Kara rolled her neck from side to side feeling the dull ache of a migraine coming on. Her mother was without a doubt one of the most stubborn people on the face of the planet. *I don't understand how someone can be so reclusive in denial about their whole life.*

"If we can't talk about this and you can't be truthful, then I can no longer associate myself with you, because this is absolutely ridiculous."

"Fine. You may leave my home."

"You'd rather end our relationship than talk to me about this situation?" Kara gazed at her mother in disbelief. "What kind of a mother are you?" Sorrowful brown eyes met angry violet ones.

"Apparently not yours, I take it. Please leave, now."

Silently moving to gather her things, Kara left without saying goodbye. She no longer knew the woman in the townhome located in Georgetown.

~ ~ ~

"No explanation. None. She just let me go. Looked at me as if I were a stranger that had trespassed at her home and not her daughter."

"I'm happy to see that you returned to see me, Kara, though I do wish these were better circumstances. You know how your mother can be. She wasn't always the way she is now, believe it or not."

Kara's recent heartbreak with her mother had led her right back to the arms of Dr. Jones. Lying on her favorite chaise, she was willing to forego their differences for the time being. Part of her still felt comfortable here. This was all she knew.

"I don't believe it."

"You should. Your mother used to be young and carefree. The first time I met her, I thought, 'What a mystical magical creature.' She was very much in love with you, your father, and her pregnancy. Part of me was a little jealous of her. I could see why your father would be attracted."

"I'm sorry, that seems completely unbelievable to me." *My mother mystical and magical? I am not buying into this fantasy she wants me to see.* "I need answers, Barbara. Real, honest answers. Please give me that. Please. My mother would rather end all communication and disown me than explain what happened."

"What is it that you would like to know? I will do my best to be as honest with you as I can be."

"What happened to my brother?" Kara asked, sitting up on the chaise. "I really need to know. Was he given up for adoption? Is he alive? Did he disown our family? What?

Where is he?"

"Your brother has unfortunately passed away. Many, many years ago. He didn't live past a few hours of being born."

"Oh no. Is that why my mother never wants to discuss it?" Sadness washed over Kara.

"One can never tell with your mother, but I do know that he was murdered, the same as my daughter. He only breathed for mere minutes before he was taken from the world."

"It seems so bizarre that both of you have murdered children with the same father." Alarm bells began going off in Kara's mind. "Were they murdered because of my father's military ties?"

"Oh, Kara, your father was never in the military," came Barbara's melancholy response. "You deserve to know that."

"That can't be true. I completed research on my dad. My mother said he was assassinated, and there was a newspaper clip. I saw it."

"You can't believe everything you read and see, sweetheart. Any and everything can be tampered with. You should know that. In your line of work, I'm sure you see that kind of thing every day."

I do know that. This personal situation is clouding my thoughts and my judgment.

"Everything my mother ever told me was a lie? This cannot be. It just can't. I don't believe it."

"I can't speak on behalf of your mother. All I can tell you is what I know from my end."

"Okay. How about your daughter? I'm curious about her. You told me how your son was, but not much about your daughter. How was she murdered? If you don't mind me asking."

"I do mind you asking. I apologize, but that is something I will not disclose to anyone. Not even you."

Kara pondered for a moment, before dropping the topic. Dr. Jones was entitled to her privacy, but she couldn't help but notice the similarities when it came to her and her mother speaking about their murdered children.

"Thank you for the information about my parents. I'll be in touch."

~ ~ ~

"What are you looking for?"

"Information about my father's children."

"Why?"

"Because, Kyle, there are many more answers there. All this time I thought my dad was in the army; turns out he wasn't. My mother fabricated the few things I thought I knew about my dad. Now I realize I know next to nothing about him. My mother's story was always that my dad was assassinated, but if you're not a government official or military or someone of prominence, how can you be assassinated? It sounds to me as if he was flat out murdered, and I want to find out why. Knowing more about his other children is as good a start as any."

"I'm beginning to think you're obsessed with this."

"I am obsessed. I have every right to be. This is my

life."

"No, this is your parents' life. How do you expect to heal if you keep coming up with new information?"

"What is going on with you?" she questioned him, turning away from the computer. "Normally you support me, but ever since that night at the bar you have been acting strange. I've been meaning to discuss that with you anyway."

"Acting strange how?"

"You know how, Kyle. The whole Aaron thing."

"I was drunk, end of story."

"No, not end of story. He's picking me up later on, and I need to know that you will conduct yourself accordingly."

Kyle's face frowned up. "Do you think it is wise to go out with someone you just met? You're staying with me because someone is stalking you. Considering that we have no idea who that is I'm putting my foot down on this one and forbidding you to go out with a stranger."

"He's not a stranger. We grew up together. If you hadn't been acting like such a jerk that night at the bar I would have introduced you to him."

"How do you know you can trust him?"

"How do you know I can't? After my mother lied to me, who's to say anyone can be trusted? Look, I'm grateful for your concern, but he and I have already gone out once."

"Without you telling me? Kay A., what are you doing? You need to be more cautious."

"I am cautious. Have a little more faith in me. I know what I'm doing."

"I sure hope so, Kay A. For your own sake."

TWENTY-NINE

THE DARK HOUSE EXCITES ME AS I SILENTLY ENTER. SHE believes she is safe here. Not knowing that such a place doesn't exist for her. She thinks staying with her partner will save her; it won't. The layout of the house is familiar to me. I've cased it many times in anticipation of my checkmate. Deep in the shadows by the wall I tried the basement doorknob, but it is locked. That's surprising. I assumed she would give her partner Kyle free range of the entire house.

THIRTY

"KARA, I REALLY WISH YOU WOULD LEAVE ME BE."

"I can't do that."

"Do you want me to say thank you? Is that it?"

"No, that is not it. I would never expect anything like that from you."

"Yeah, well, thank you for not speaking at my parole hearing, and letting me be able to get out of prison early for a crime I never committed. Thank you for that."

"Ryan, please don't do this. I did what I thought was best and what I could in a situation that has been messed up from the start."

Ryan glanced around the parking lot looking for his wife. *Sophie, where are you?*

"I want to warn you, Sophie is not who she appears to be. Trust me on this."

"I'm not going to do this with you today. Please leave."

"Just hear me out. Please, Ryan, a few minutes. Nothing more."

Sophie pulled up just as Kara was about to tell Ryan what she had found out. Kara watched as he entered the car with his wife and left her in the parking lot. Kara intentionally drove to North Carolina to be waiting when he stepped out of the jail. Taking a much-needed break from the drama in her life, she was going to warn Ryan as much as she could about the information she discovered.

Following behind the car, Kara was determined that Ryan was going to hear her out tonight. Pulling into the same driveway the candy-apple-red BMW had driven up Kara jumped out of the car.

"Kara, this is ridiculous. Go home."

"I'm too far to just go home. Please just hear me out. I only need a few minutes of your time."

"No. It's been a long day. I'm going to lie down. Good night." Ryan strolled toward the house before gazing at Sophie. "I forgot, I don't have a key. Can you let me in?"

"Of course, honey." She ran to the door, unlocking it so he could enter.

"Sophie?" Kara called out. The woman hesitated before making the decision to walk over to her.

"How can I help you?"

"I'm—"

"I know who you are. Both Ryan and my dad told me all about you. What I'm having a hard time understanding is why you have shown up here at my home at all."

"I'm here to warn Ryan about you and your father."

"Warn Ryan about us?" Sophie questioned in shocked disbelief. "You're the one that needs to walk around with a warning sign on your chest explaining to people how dangerous you are."

"Excuse me?" Kara was visibly taken back.

"We know all about you, Kara Anthony. All about your little hit and run. Leaving Ryan to take the fall for your neglectful actions and behavior."

"He told you about that?"

"Yes, he did. I'm his wife. Why wouldn't he tell me about that?"

"Did you tell Ryan who you are?"

"I don't know what you are referring to."

"Oh, I think you do know. Does Ryan know that you are the sister of the boy from the accident that day?"

"I have no idea what you're speaking about."

"Don't play coy with me. You know exactly what I'm speaking about. The problem is Ryan doesn't know. I would like to know when you plan to tell him. Why did you seek him out? Because long before he told you about me, you had come around. What are your motives?"

"Whatever they are is of no concern of yours."

"That's where you have it wrong. Ryan and his safety are very much a concern of mine."

"I hate you. Please leave my home before I call the police, and I will be making sure that my father is aware of your unwelcome visit at my home."

"I don't take threats very well."

"It's a promise, Detective. I'm sure you know what those are."

"Kara, why are you still here?" Ryan had come back to the door, calling out to the woman glaring at his wife in the yard. "Sophie, come inside. I'll handle her."

"There is no need, honey. Your little friend here will be returning to DC tonight."

"Ryan, she's the sister of the kid that died that night in the accident. You can't trust her," Kara yelled from the driveway. She wasn't leaving until she said what she had come to say.

Ryan stared at her baffled. "What are you blabbering

about?"

"Don't listen to her, darling. She is clearly delusional. It's your first night home. Let me draw you a hot bath."

"Don't trust her, Ryan. I'm pleading with you," Kara kept yelling.

Ryan turned to Sophie. "Is what she's saying true?"

"Yes, it is."

"You lied to me."

"But hold on. At first I sought you out because I was curious about you, and then I came to love you. Once you told me the story about you, Kara, and the accident, I realized you were a victim, a pawn in her little game. She's the one you can't trust, baby. She could've told you all of this in a letter, but she never wrote you, not one time while you were locked up. She only began visiting you when it was beneficial and convenient for her. That's not the type of friend you need. Mark my words, babe, you can't trust her."

Kara had to give it to Sophie, she was smart and had no intention of backing down whatsoever.

"Ryan, despite all of that, please believe me."

Ryan turned an icy glare on Kara. "I have to agree with my wife. Good night, Kara. Please get home safely and don't come again. You aren't welcome here."

Sophie smiled smugly at her as the duo retreated inside leaving Kara in the driveway appearing as she was: an unwanted,   uninvited   guest.

THIRTY-ONE

"RISE AND SHINE, BEAUTIFUL."

"Why? Is it morning already?" Kara whined. "I need a few more hours of sleep."

"If you would stop spending your nights casing the streets like a ghost rider, you might feel better. I would feel better. At the risk of sounding like a broken record, you have a stalker somewhere," Kyle reminded her. "Did you take care of whatever it was that couldn't wait?"

"Not exactly," Kara responded. "What time is it?"

"5:17."

"A.M.? Kyle, I'm still suspended. There is no reason for me to be up at such an ungodly hour." Pulling the covers back over her head, "I'm going back to sleep," Kara stated.

"I have information on your dad."

The covers come back down on the bed immediately.

"What kind of information?" Kara opened one sleepy eye.

"I figured that would pique your interest."

"Come, sit." Kara patted the mattress next to her, refusing to sit up or open her other eye.

"That may be a little too close," Kyle joked. "Your morning breath may kill me, and I didn't sign up to register in the morgue today." Kyle was genuinely amusing himself.

Kara's jovial laugh echoed through the basement. "My breath may be a little tart, but it will not kill you, stop it.

Now sit. What type of information are you sitting on, my favorite detective?"

"Wouldn't you like to know?"

"Yes, I would. Now cough it up."

"After doing some digging, I found the head homicide detective that handled your father's case."

"Are you serious?" Kara was taken by surprise.

"I am. He's retired now, but he's willing to speak with us."

"Kyle, this is amazing news. I'm excited. How soon is he willing to speak with us?"

"Right now. I invited him over. He's upstairs."

"What? This early?"

"Yes Kay A. Enough questions. Get dressed, let's go."

"Aye, aye, Captain." Kara saluted him.

"You're such the comedian. Be upstairs in five." He left her so she could get dressed.

Approximately five minutes later Kara was walking into the den as the two men halted their conversation and stood.

"Hello."

"So glad you could join us. Sleeping Beauty has risen." Kyle laughed. "Kara, this is George Brown. He was the lead investigator on your father's case."

"It's a pleasure to meet you, Mr. Brown." Kara reached out to shake his hand. "Please, please sit." She motioned for the older man to return to the seat he'd vacated once she entered. His calm demeanor was strong and demanded one's respect. Not quite a twin of the actor Morgan

Freeman, but he could pass as a first or second cousin.

"The pleasure is mine," he stated.

"I'm anxious to hear about the work done on my father's case. What do you know?"

"What we know is that the firearm used to murder your father was an APR 308. It can shoot up to 1,094 yards. The shot was very accurate. If it helps you feel better, he didn't suffer."

Kara nodded as he continued.

"Of course you know his murder has gone unsolved for the past twenty years."

"Yes, I am well aware. I don't know if Kyle filled you in, but I have a stalker. The closer we get to the anniversary of my father's death, the more intense things have become for me. After discovering my half-sister was murdered and something happened to my baby brother, something my mother vehemently refuses to address, I believe whoever murdered him twenty years ago is coming back for me now."

"Little lady, I'd watch myself out here if I were you. There were no leads in this case. So no one will know who is after you and how to protect you from them."

"Do you have old case files I can comb through?"

"No, I got rid of those files years ago."

How strange. Since when do people get rid of case files?

"Is there any other information you can share with me? Did you interview my mom, or my dad's wife? His friends? Anyone?"

"I've shared with you all I can. I do believe it is time for me to be heading out." Mr. Brown stood, forcing Kara and Kyle to do the same.

"Thank you for stopping by, Mr. Brown. Please take care."

Kyle walked Mr. Brown out as Kara watched from the window. He handed Mr. Brown a white envelope before Mr. Brown entered his car.

This whole situation doesn't seem right.

"Why did you invite him here? He didn't tell us anything we didn't already know except for what type of weapon was used." Kyle had just returned from outside.

"I thought he would give you more information."

"What kind of detective are you, Whitlock? Always ask questions first, please. You know this already, especially if you're going to be waking me up at such an ungodly hour." She smacked him in the arm. "I'm going back to bed."

Can I trust Kyle?

Back in bed staring at the ceiling Kara couldn't put her mind at ease. She was sure some sort of game was being played that she was at the center of, and now she knew for a fact that in order to stay alive the rules were trust no one.

THIRTY-TWO

VICTORIA SAT ON THE COLD, UNWELCOMING GROUND, STARING at the elephantine tombstone. "My husband, my love, my friend, Charles Lee Anthony 1957–1997" it read. Taunting her, even in his death, Barbara had the upper hand.

"If you were here, I know you would understand, Chuck. You are the love of my life. After your murder, everything else ceased to matter to me. Including your cupcake. I don't know why I adopted that name for her too; that's your name for her. I resent myself for so many reasons, Chuck. The reasons are too numerous to count. Now your cupcake is requesting information about what happened to her brother, and I'm at a loss for words of what to say to her. I miss you. I wish a miracle could bring you back to me, but I know miracles don't exist." The chill in the morning air forced her to pull her shoulder wrap tighter around her body.

"Fancy seeing you here."

So consumed in her thoughts of she and Charles, Victoria hadn't heard anyone approach. She lifted her head at the sound of the familiar voice. "It's his birthday. I always spend it with him."

"Funny, so do I. That's what widowers do," the voice taunted her.

"I came here for peace, Barbara," Victoria sighed, "and clarity. Not to fight with you for the rest of eternity about a man that didn't love either one of us as much as he loved himself."

"That's where you are wrong. There was love all in our

relationship. That's why I don't understand why there was you."

"Oh, you understand why. You may be in denial, but you understand it." *So much for peace.*

A pregnant pause went by before either woman spoke.

"Kara returned to see me. I told her about her brother and that he only lived for a few hours before he passed away."

"You didn't have to do that."

"I know. I was hoping it would help her not have to choose between the two of us. It's been a long time, Victoria. Let's move on from this. It has done nothing but make us both bitter and harbor resentment toward one another."

Staring off into the distance, Victoria knew she was right. It was time to let go. Charles had been gone for almost twenty years, and the two of them were holding on as if he were coming back tomorrow.

"You're right."

"Well, wonders will never cease to amaze me. Did you just say that I was right?" Her sarcasm garnered a smile from Victoria. In another life, perhaps she and Barbara could have been friends.

"Try not to gloat so much, okay? I'm just tired of all this bickering between the two of us."

"You and me both."

The two sat in their first comfortable silence together.

Barbara cleared her throat. "I also told Kara that her father was never in the military. I'm surprised she believed that lie as long as she did, but I felt it wasn't right to keep her in the dark. She needed to know."

"I'm not surprised. I fed her that information her whole life. The child is practically brainwashed when it comes to her father. I wanted her to think he was an amazing man, not one with two separate families. She needed a hero to look up to."

"She has you. You could be the hero for her instead of casting her out of your life."

Victoria was surprised. "She told you that as well, huh?"

Barber nodded. "Yes, she did. She needs you right now as she deals with all of this new information."

"I can't deal with her right now. She only seeks answers about her brother, and that's a topic I don't want to speak about. Ever."

"She asked me about Kellie as well."

"I'm not surprised. My cupcake is persistently inquisitive." Victoria's voice hinted surprisingly of pride. "What did you tell her?"

"That the topic wasn't up for discussion."

"That was very Victoria of you."

"Very." Barbara copped a squat next to Victoria. "Does this mean we can finally be cordial with one another moving forward?"

"Yes, we can be cordial."

"Thank you, Victoria. Thank you."

THIRTY-THREE

"SINCE MISTY DROPPED HER COMPLAINT, ANY WORD ON MY suspension being lifted? I'm anxious to get back on the job." *And not deal with my personal life.*

"Job? You no longer have a job. You killed my boy. Do you honestly think I would let you back in here after that?"

"What?"

"So now something is wrong with your hearing?"

Kara had heard just fine. The problem was she hadn't expected him to come right out and accuse her.

"No, Captain, my hearing is fine." She proceeded with caution. One could never know what someone is capable of once emotions are involved.

"Good. You're being transferred after you are removed from administrative leave. Your suspension is already lifted. Not by my call. But even I must answer to someone. Now get out of my office. If I ever see you again it will be too soon."

Kara knew how he knew about her, but he must have known that for a while. What she couldn't understand is why he never spoke on it until now.

"Before I leave, I want to extend an apology to you. I was young and foolish." Tears marred Kara's eyes. "I wish there was something, anything I could do to fix this. I didn't know until you put me on that case that you were his father."

"I asked you to leave." The captain's icy tongue hit her ears like a glacier. "You will get what's coming to you. I guarantee it."

Hastily exiting the room, Kara knew a threat when she heard one. Except this time, it rang more as a promise.

THIRTY-FOUR

SHE'S ENTIRELY TOO SMART FOR HER OWN GOOD. THAT daughter of mine. If she would stop quoting me, we could go back to being mother and daughter. Opening the door to the dimly lit basement, she barely walked down the five stairs that it took to enter her basement fully, before she tripped over a doggy bowl filled with water. As she fell to the plush carpet knees first, she was grateful she had the basement remodeled the previous year to place the carpet over the hardwood floors that had previously been down.

Glancing around the room as she pushed herself up right, she was confused. *How did this bowl make its way to the bottom of my steps?* Reaching for the flashlight she kept on a shelf next to the stairs, she slowly began walking around, the ray of light guiding her. *I really need to put lights down here.* Moving the light from side to side she finally saw what she was looking for: Lucifer, her black and brown Doberman pinscher. He was sitting in the corner staring intently into a box she kept down there.

"What's wrong, Lucifer? Come here, boy." He turned his head when he heard his name, then slowly made his way to her, placing a paw on her foot.

"Good boy." Victoria rubbed behind his ears. "You trying to kill Momma?" she whispered to him. "You can't leave your bowl at the bottom of the stairs, okay?" she scolded lightly. "Now come, time for dinner."

Victoria placed the flashlight back on the shelf as the

content duo made their way up the stairs toward the kitchen.

"Lucifer, your sister has been disowned. She's entirely too busy meddling in business that is none of hers." Victoria cut up the freshly prepared steak as Lucifer sat calmly at her feet watching her slice the meat. "Why won't she leave the past in the past? Huh, boy?"

Lucifer gazed at Victoria as she spoke, patiently waiting for his dinner. Victoria placed the steak on a glass plate and set it on the floor. *Only the best for my baby.* She rubbed him behind the ears as again he leaned into her touch, proceeding to sniff his dinner before taking a bite.

Satisfied that he was well taken care of Victoria exited the kitchen to go into her office, which was the next door over.

Pulling a book off the bookcase, she sat in the leather chair behind her desk. *Oh, my dear boy, how I used to read you these wonderful stories. You loved when your mama would do that, didn't you?* She picked up the photo of when her son was a few hours old, that she'd hidden in the book. *So perfect, my little one.* So much for what could have been. *Enough of this self-pity, Victoria. Stop it!* Placing the photo back into the book, she returned the book to its place, letting go of what could have been, looking forward to the future.

THIRTY-FIVE

A WEEK AFTER KARA'S UNTIMELY POP IN NORTH CAROLINA, Ryan had tried ignoring the nagging feeling he had.

"I didn't know you were the sister of the kid in my case. Why would you hold something like that back from me?" Ryan was upset. He thought he knew Sophie, but it was obvious no one ever really knew anyone in life. Kara, the first woman he'd ever loved, had abandoned him; Sophie, the second love of his life, was a deceitful liar. He couldn't win for losing.

"Ryan, darling, you really shouldn't concern yourself with such trivial matters. The hows and whys are irrelevant. All that's important is that we were able to find one another."

"No, Sophie, it absolutely matters. I have to be able to trust you."

Sophie flashed an award-winning smile his way. "Baby, of course you can trust me. You trusted me last night," she said, her voice seductive, "and you loved every moment of it."

"I've been locked up for five years. Of course I loved it. That was sex; enjoyable, but still sex. Today I need answers," he told her sternly.

"Fine," Sophie gave in. "I didn't tell you because I wanted to avoid this conversation that we are having right now."

"Don't you think it would have come up at some point

in our marriage?"

"I was going to cross that bridge when we got to it."

"Well we're here, so begin crossing." Ryan was impatient. "Why did you seek me out? Is this some sick joke? Some old revenge scores you're trying to settle?"

Sophie smiled. Ryan thought it sinister how her smile resembled that of the Joker.

"It's already been settled."

"What do you mean? Ho—"

The first bullet caught him in the gut; the next one in the shoulder.

"See." Sophie's eyes flashed excitedly in the sunlight shining through the room, watching a desperate Ryan trying to breathe as his body fell to the floor. "It's been settled." She kneeled down next to him as blood began easing out of his mouth. Their eyes locked together.

"My brother meant the world to me. You may not have killed him, but you were there that night. Because of you and her, I grew up alone." Sophie stood and exited the room as the gurgling sounds slowly ceased.

"It's done," Sophie said into the phone as she grabbed her car keys, leaving North Carolina forever.

THIRTY-SIX

"WELCOME TO MY HUMBLE ABODE."

Kara was vastly impressed. Aaron lived in a high-rise condo at the National Harbor in Oxon Hill, Maryland, with a phenomenal view that overlooked the Potomac River and Washington, DC.

"Wow, the city looks so amazing at night."

"It's one of the main reasons I purchased this place. I love to stand at the window and paint."

"You're a painter?"

"More like an amateur playing with watercolors, but I get the job done."

"How very modest of you. I'm sure they're fabulous paintings."

Kara looked around his condo taking everything in. Though it was not large, what it lacked in size, it made up with style.

Aaron's aesthetic was simplistic yet masculine. His condo was painted in grays, blues, and whites. His floor-to-ceiling windows that overlooked the city had white curtains that were pulled open to expose the view of the city. His cherry minibar was completely stocked, though she didn't expect anything less from a bartender. *How can he afford all of this?* His entertainment system was impressive in size, taking up an entire wall equipped with a 70" curved TV and a PlayStation. *Men and their toys.*

"This is a lovely bachelor's pad. I could never afford a place like this in a million years. It takes all my pennies to upkeep my townhouse."

Aaron only smiled in response to her statement, not taking the bate of how he sustained.

"I've got a surprise for you."

"Really?"

"Follow me." Kara fell in line behind him as he guided her to the massive windows. Then smiled. There on the floor was a blanket, two wine glasses, a bowl of caesar salad, a plate of roasted lamb with asparagus and rice pilaf; a bottle of Chardonnay and a small bowl of strawberries.

"What is all of this?"

"A dinner for two."

"I can see that. Wow. Are you ever the romantic."

"Sit with me."

"I'd love to." Kara removed her shoes, wiggling her bare toes on his soft carpet.

As the two sat on the floor, Aaron reached for her hand, bowing his head as he said grace. Kara followed his lead.

"Now let's begin."

Using an electric corkscrew, he opened the wine, pouring it into both glasses.

"Aaron, where have you been all my life? This is amazing."

"I've been in the background waiting for you to notice me."

"Lies." She smiled

"Truth. Cross my heart and hope to die."

Laughing at their long-ago kiddie ritual, Kara took a bite of her salad.

"I've always had a crush on you. Since the very beginning."

"You never said anything."

"In high school you had your sweetheart already, everyone knew it."

"Ryan was my sweetheart. I ruined his life though, so maybe it's better that we didn't reconnect until now."

"How could you ruin anyone's life?"

"Trust me, there are ways," Kara told him before shoving more salad into her mouth.

"I'll take your word for it."

She nodded as they ate in silence.

"Dessert?"

"Oh no. I cannot stuff another bite of food into my mouth. You will be rolling me out of here if I do."

"Okay, so let's talk."

"Let's."

"My sister found more information she wants to share with you. She'll only tell you. I have no clue what she found."

"Please tell your sister thank you for me. You two are being very kind to help me like this."

"It's no problem. Really. I can't imagine your life after that day. I'll help in any way possible."

"Aaron, you are nothing short of wonderful."

It was Aaron's turn to blush.

"Thank you."

"Can I ask you a few questions about that day?"

"Sure." Aaron knew the exact day she was referencing.

"What do you remember happening while we were outside. Everything is a blur to me. I was in shock, but do you remember anything?"

"Not too much. When your dad got out of the car, the shooting began almost immediately. Whoever did it knew he would be there at that time."

"It doesn't add up. I distinctly remember my mother telling me that he wouldn't be coming till the next day, and then he must've changed his mind to come a day earlier. How would the shooter know that? My mother and I didn't even know until a few minutes before he pulled up."

"You're right, it doesn't add up."

"What is it that I'm missing?" Kara was deep in thought when she heard her cell phone begin to vibrate. Reaching for her purse, she pulled the phone out, frowning at the unknown number.

"Hello," she answered. "Oh no, when? How? I'm on my way."

"What is it?" Aaron could tell something bad had happened.

"That was North Carolina's Homicide Department. Ryan has been murdered." Kara jumped up practically running out the door. "I have to go."

"Wait," Aaron called after her, "I'm coming with you."

THIRTY-SEVEN

"THIS WAY."

Kara arrived on the scene in a record two hours, catching the next flight out of Washington DC to Raleigh. Following behind the detective, she was trying her best to follow his pace and not pass him in a rush to get to Ryan's body.

I tried to warn you, Ryan. Why wouldn't you listen?

They entered the room where his body lay. A sheet had been placed over him. Kara braced herself for what she would see as the sheet was lifted.

Oh, Ryan. There lay her high school sweetheart with his eyes still open, a forlorn expression on his face. *You never stood a chance.* She wiped the lone tear that had escaped from her eye. *I knew there wasn't something right about Sophie. No one lets go of those type of grudges easily, and I know she's coming for me next.*

"You can't take cases like this personal," Chief Chase, the head of the Raleigh, North Carolina, police department told Kara as he patted her back.

It is personal.

"The reason we called you is because we found this note with your name and number on it." He handed Kara an envelope with her name written across the front. "We found it taped to the back of the chest in the bedroom."

My poor Ryan, your life is over and it's all my fault.

Walking away from his body and out of the house he'd shared only a few days with Sophie, Kara entered her rented Jeep waiting for her in the driveway that Aaron was driving. He'd insisted on driving her to North Carolina when she had given him the news about Ryan. He'd waited patiently in the car because he was unauthorized to access a crime scene, the same way she would have been if Raleigh PD knew she was on administrative leave from her department and in the process of being transferred.

"You alright?"

Shaking her head no, Kara tore open the seal of the envelope.

Kara,

I have this gnawing feeling that you were right. Ever since that night you showed up, everything has been different. Sophie is different. If she didn't mean me harm, why would she keep the family association a secret from me? The vibe is off with us. She's plotting something. I came to town briefly, but no one was at your house. Where are you? Something bad is going to happen to me. I want you to know that I love you. I have always loved you. I wish that awful night had never happened. I wonder what we would be doing right now. Maybe we'd have a couple of children. Who knows? Me playing football probably and you being the magnificent detective that you are. How could I forget how brilliant you are? Of course you knew Sophie was dangerous. You tried to help me. I let my anger cloud my judgment. If you're reading this letter it means that I am dead; but I get to do this last good deed. She will be after you next, so watch your back. She's coming, and she may be bringing her dad along. How is that job going anyway?

Love always,

Ryan

"This is not fair. Ryan did not deserve any of this."

"Tell me what happened."

Kara explained her and Ryan's situation to Aaron, passing him the note so he could read that as well.

"You're right, he didn't deserve it, but you can't blame yourself for this either. You aren't the one who killed him."

"I know, but my actions years ago set the stage for this tragedy to happen. He was safer in jail." Kara punched the dashboard in anger. "She will pay for this."

THIRTY-EIGHT

"YOU MIND TELLING ME WHERE YOU HAVE BEEN?"

Kara barely had both feet in the door before Kyle was quizzing her. She actually didn't mind, but with his little attitude it didn't exactly make her want to tell him either.

"Miss me much?" Her sarcastic comment was met with Kyle's inscrutable stare. "Okay, okay. I had to fly to North Carolina."

"Does your phone not work?"

"Why are you so angry? I was unaware that I needed to check in with you first about my whereabouts."

Kyle was seething mad. The last Kara had told him was that she was going out with Aaron; that had been two days ago.

"No one is saying you have to check in, but you are running around town as if your safety is of no concern to you. Someone is stalking you. Why must I keep reminding you of the danger that *you're* in?"

"I am well aware, because you won't let me forget. But I can't live in a box, Kyle, just sitting in this house waiting for someone to pounce on me, either."

Kyle regarded her in tormented silence. Sometimes she could be so headstrong. He almost wanted to strangle her himself, until she learned to listen.

"When were you going to tell me that your suspension had been lifted and you were being transferred?"

Aha. The root of his anger. "I planned to tell you just as soon as I had a mome—." The lights suddenly going out cut Kara's sentence short. "What's going on?"

Kyle glanced out the window to see that all of his neighbors still had lights.

"You think a fuse blew?" Deep down she knew that wasn't it.

"No," Kyle stated matter-of-factly, confirming her fear. "You got your piece on you?" he whispered into the darkness.

"Of course." Kara pulled her 9mm out of her waistband.

"Good, get down," Kyle instructed.

Kara was already lying down flat on the floor trying to see if she heard any noises, be it outside or in. She could make out Kyle's silhouette thanks to the help of the moonlight filtering through the windows.

"I don't hear anything."

"Me either."

That's when they both heard the unmistakable sound of footsteps passing by the window. Kara kept her hand steady as she waited. The footsteps paused outside the door for a brief second before continuing around the house.

Kara hated feeling like a sitting duck, yet that's exactly what she and Kyle were as they sat waiting for the unknown to occur.

That can't be what I think it is. "Do you smell that?" Kara sniffed the air. It had been roughly ten minutes since they'd last heard footsteps.

Kyle followed suit sniffing the air. "It smells like kerosene."

"And smoke. Somethings on fire." They both stood in unison, keeping close to the walls, before flames shot up outside the window.

"We have to get out of here."

Kara threw the front door open, only to immediately jump back and slam it as the smoke and flames threatened to choke and burn her.

"Let's try the back."

"Okay, you lead the way. I'll stay close on your back," she told Kyle.

The two soon realized that going out the back was as futile as trying to go through the front. Flames engulfed all entryways and exits to the house.

"How are we going to get out of here?" Kara coughed, covering her nose with the sleeve of her shirt.

"We can either try through the basement, but that's probably blocked as well by now, or we can go upstairs and jump from the second floor. If neither of those sound good, we can wet our entire bodies and run through the flames."

Wet ourselves? Kyle is crazy. We don't have time for that.

"We're going to have to use our stop, drop, and roll abilities because we're going through the front. Let's go. Stay close in case the pyro is still here."

"Kay A., wait."

"No, we don't have time to wait. Now! We're going now."

Kara ran toward the front door with Kyle close on her heels. The entire house was now filled with smoke. Kara knew it was only a matter of time before they both suffered from smoke inhalation. As Kara threw open the front door, the dancing flames were frightening, but she saw no other option. She'd rather try her hand going through it versus dying in the house from not doing anything.

Here goes nothing. She pulled her shirt over her head to protect her hair from catching fire and made a dash for it as fast as she could go through the flames to the oxygen haven of the front yard. She could only hope Kyle was somewhere close behind.

Grateful to have made it through the flames she immediately dropped to the ground and began rolling around in the grass, determined to eliminate the fire embracing her clothes. *I made it.* She inhaled the night air deeply, her oxygen-deprived lungs rejoicing in appreciation as the sirens in the distance began to get louder. *Where is Kyle?*

Rolling to her feet, Kara looked around with her gun withdrawn. That's when she saw him lying on the ground, flames overtaking his body.

"KYLE!" she yelled, removing her shirt, attempting to fight the flames engulfing him. "Kyle, can you hear me?"

He moaned in response. *At least that's something.* Kara continued trying to douse the flames until the fire department, police, and EMTs arrived.

"We'll take it from here, ma'am."

Kara backed away to give them space to work as the firemen connected their hose to the fire hydrant and began dousing the house in water. By the time they were done,

Kyle was on his way to the hospital and the house left something to be desired, a shell of its former self.

I cannot believe this. Kara shook her head as she took in the massive mess sitting in front of her. That's when she saw it, sitting on the edge of the property close to the neighbor's house, gleaming in the darkness: a bouquet of white roses.

Can't be. In a trance, she made a beeline for the bouquet. Reaching for the note propped on the vase, Kara looked around to see if anyone was watching her before she opened it.

Time is winding down. You may have survived this far, but all it takes is one time, for the lights to go out forever. Tick, tick, tick goes the clock.

I'm watching you.

THIRTY-NINE

"YOU'RE PRETTY LUCKY, YOU KNOW?"

"Yes, I know." Kara had finally made her way to the hospital to get looked over by the doctor after the fire incident at Kyle's house.

"A few minor burns and that's all. Your friend wasn't so lucky."

"He's a tough guy. I know he'll be okay," Kara told the doctor as she picked up her purse preparing to leave.

"You're pretty tough yourself. Make sure you go home and rest."

"I will check on my friend first and then do exactly as you say," Kara assured the doctor.

"Good to hear. Any problems, please give me a call as soon as possible."

"Duly noted," Kara replied as she left the room.

Walking to the third floor where the burn unit was located Kara stopped by the reception desk to inquire about Kyle's room assignment, when she noticed a familiar face sitting in the relatively empty visiting area.

"Barbara?"

Dr. Jones glanced up from the magazine she was reading.

"Kara, hi. What are you doing here?"

"My partner and I were ambushed at his house tonight. He has a few bad burns."

"I'm sorry to hear that." Her face was lined with concern.

"He's a trooper. I know he'll be just fine."

"Glad to hear it."

"Nice seeing you, Dr. Jones."

"Likewise, Kara, likewise."

Kara left Dr. Jones in the waiting area to peek her head into Kyle's room.

"If you needed a few days off, I'm sure the captain would have approved it. No need to go to such extremes," Kara joked as she leaned down to place a gentle kiss on Kyle's forehead. Her friend's arms were bandaged up, and his head was wrapped.

"It's too soon for jokes. I'm not ready yet," Kyle grimaced.

"You, my friend, have seen better days." Kara caressed the side of his face.

"Don't I know it." Kyle opened his eyes long enough to take in Kara's appearance.

"How is it you look fine and I've been admitted to the hospital?"

"I'm a professional," she kidded him. "Don't despair, you'll get there one day."

"You're mighty jolly. Where's the sympathy?"

"You getting soft on me, Whitlock?"

"I'll never be soft."

Kara laughed. "I do have some news."

"Oh yeah, what's that?"

"I found another bouquet of white roses and card once the fire was out."

"Roses, at my house?"

"Yes."

"Great, we know your stalker found you at my place. This is exactly why I tell you to be careful."

"I know, I know. But now that your house is a disaster, we have to return to mine."

"I feel that if we do that we will be playing right into your stalker's hand. This whole thing was staged to get you to go back to your house, I guarantee it."

"I know, but where else is there to go? My mother isn't speaking to me. Your house is a roast fest. My home is where we are going. We will have to just stay on our p's and q's until my father's death anniversary arrives. Whatever is going to go down will happen that day. We only need to be ready."

"If you say so, Kay A. You're the boss."

"If you say so, Whitlock. I'm about to get out of here."

"Do not go to your house until I am released from here."

"Kyle, I have to go."

"You promise me, Anthony. Right now, or I'm leaving this hospital with you."

"You will do no such thing. Get your rest. I promise you I will go nowhere near my own home until you are released."

"Is that your word?"

"Yes, it is. I already have plans to stay with a friend tonight."

"What friend would that be? The one from the bar?"

"Kyle, let's not go into that, okay? Get some rest. I'll be back tomorrow to visit you." She leaned down again to place another kiss on his forehead. "Good night."

FORTY

"THANK YOU FOR LETTING ME STAY HERE TONIGHT. I REALLY appreciate it."

"You are always welcome here."

"You're the best, Aaron, and I mean that. A true godsend."

"Don't make me blush." Aaron pulled Kara along the full length of his body. "I've been waiting to do this since I saw you in my bar that night."

Kara gazed at his full lips as they descended upon hers. The heat they transferred to one another was hotter than the flamed house she'd recently escaped.

"I'm glad you're okay. I just found you again. I can't lose you."

"Today has been such a long day. First Ryan's death, then the fire. Why is a day of peace so hard to come by?" *God, are you ignoring me?*

"I don't have an answer to that, but I can give you a massage to make you feel better."

"A massage would be very, very lovely," Kara stated.

"I give the best ones." Aaron scooped Kara up into his arms and carried her into his bedroom, placing her gently in the middle of his king-sized therapeutic bed.

"I'ma hold you to that, mister."

"Please do. Now, I'm going to take you out of all your clothes."

"Is that right?"

"Absolutely."

Aaron proceeded to ease Kara's clothes off her body. Then he left her in bed as he drew a fresh bath for her before returning to the bed to carry her to the warm water freshly loaded into the bathtub.

"I love bubble baths."

"Glad to hear it."

Aaron bathed Kara in silence, allowing her body to enter complete relaxation mode. As he continued washing her he noticed her breathing had changed. She had fallen asleep.

Pulling a towel from the towel rack, Aaron placed it over her and lifted her up into his arms, out of the cooling water. Her head fell onto his chest as her hair softly draped over his arm.

Turning down the comforter on the bed with one hand, he lowered her onto the cool sheets, covering her nudity with the comforter. Turning the light off in his bedroom, Aaron closed the door, opting to sleep on the sofa.

Kara woke the next morning feeling better than she should. *Where am I?* She stared at the unfamiliar ceiling until memories began flooding back. Ryan's murder, the fire at Kyle's, Kyle in the hospital, Aaron picking her up.

I'm at Aaron's. Sitting up in the bed, the covers fell to her waist. She was surprised to find herself completely nude. *What happened last night?*

Seeing one of Aaron's T-shirts on a chair, she hastily put it on before leaving the room. Upon walking out, Kara stopped and smiled as Aaron lay on the sofa slumbering as peacefully as a small child, cuddling his pillow.

Leaving him to his fairyland, Kara made herself at home in the kitchen. His refrigerator was stocked to capacity. Retrieving a pack of bacon, eggs, and pancake mix, Kara set about the task of putting her domestic skills to use.

Aaron opened his eyes smelling the sweet aroma of food calling out his name. *Time to get up.* "What's going on in my kitchen?"

Kara's breath caught at Aaron braced on the door frame in nothing but pajama pants, displaying an impressive set of abs and a lazy smile.

"Breakfast is cooking, sleepy head."

Kara cut off the stove burner as she placed the last pancake on a plate resting on the kitchen table.

"Come and get it."

"Is that an open invitation?" Aaron's intense gaze leveled on Kara's bare legs peeking out from beneath his T-shirt as he waited for her response.

"Maybe." Kara eluded, not one to back down from the challenge she saw in Aaron's eyes.

"Come here." Aaron held out a hand to her.

Kara knew what he wanted. She had to make a decision.

Walking over to him, she pulled his T-shirt up and off of her toned body; happy that she spent so much time running so her physique was impeccable; taking his hand. This was by far one of the easiest decisions she had ever made in her life.

The lovemaking that ensued was ground shattering by

all accounts. Kara had the feeling she could get addicted to Aaron, and an addiction to anything was dangerous— especially in her life right now.

Breakfast was cold by the time they returned to the table smiling into each other's eyes. The shrill ringing of Kara's cell phone broke the magic spell that swirled around the room. A sense of doomed déjà vu drifted over her when she saw Jason's name flashing on her LCD screen.

"Jason, what is it? You have got to be kidding me. Okay, I'll be there right away." Hanging up the phone swiftly, she turned to Aaron, regretful to leave their cozy atmosphere.

"What's going on?" Aaron asked, hearing the urgency in her tone.

Kara began speed walking toward the bedroom to clothe herself, beginning to wonder if Aaron's place was a magnet for bad news.

"My ex-fiancé's wife, Misty, is missing."

FORTY-ONE

"WHAT HAPPENED?" KARA ARRIVED TO JASON AND MISTY'S brand-new Accokeek home in record time considering the National Harbor was only fifteen minutes away. Kara had entered the mini-mansion in full-on detective mode as if she were the head of the investigation. But she couldn't miss the extravagance of his home. It was a far cry from his condo in Alexandria.

"Misty left for her morning run yesterday, and I haven't heard from or seen her since."

"You let a full twenty-four hours pass before contacting anyone?" Kara was perplexed and stunned.

Jason could be so aloof and out of touch sometimes. She hadn't seen either of the two since she'd handed Misty over to the police when they were all in Dr. Jones's office.

"Misty and I have been at odds lately. I figured she needed time to let off some steam, but when I noticed her cell phone still here and she didn't returned home last night nor this morning, I knew something must be wrong."

"Why call me and not the police?"

"Because you know us personally and will make sure things are handled expeditiously."

"Jason, I'm still on administrative leave and in the process of being transferred. You're going to have to hand this case over to the local authorities. I don't want to lie to you, but when you do contact them there's a very likely chance that you will turn into a prime suspect. You have a motive, and your alibi is what? You were waiting at home for your wife's return like a dutiful little husband?"

"I didn't do anything to Misty. I'm worried about her. That's why I called you." Jason's face was one of worry.

"I understand that, but I have to report this in case Misty is in any real danger. Unless you call and report it yourself. Right now."

"I'll do whatever it is you think I should do, Kara. I just want Misty to be okay."

"Call the police. Right now."

She watched as Jason did as he was told.

"Great, the police will be here soon. There's somewhere I have to be."

"Okay. Thank you for coming by so quickly. I love you for that."

"I was in the area. No skin off my back. Good luck on your search. Be sure to keep me updated."

"I will."

FORTY-TWO

"READY TO MARCH OUT OF HERE, HANDSOME?"

"You're late."

"Well, good morning to you too."

"Where have you been?"

"What happened to my old cheery buddy Kyle? This new Kyle has an attitude. Please bring my old Kyle back."

Kyle smiled sheepishly. "Am I becoming a shrew?"

Kara held her thumb and forefinger close together. "A little bit. Nothing I can't handle, however, which is lucky for you."

Once Kara got Kyle home, she filled him in.

"What has been going on since I last saw you?" Kyle asked Kara once they were back at her house and he was settled into the guest room.

"Everything." Kara sat on the end of the bed. "When I got home yesterday, I never had the opportunity to tell you that Ryan was murdered and I think Sophie and Captain Harris had a hand in it."

"Captain Harris?" Kyle shook his head in disbelief. "Why would he put you on the case if he and his daughter were going to do something like this?"

"He wanted me to know he knew I was the one guilty and that he was going to make sure I paid for it."

"All of this is surreal."

"I know. That's why I was in Raleigh yesterday, but as soon as I got back the fire broke out. Then this morning Jason called me to alert me to the fact that Misty is missing."

"Is the world trying to end? What in God's green earth is going on?"

"That's what I keep asking myself."

"Who's that?" Kyle asked as the doorbell rang.

"Aaron."

"Aaron, huh? Are you two an official item now? You've been seeing him a lot."

"No, Kyle, we're not. He's bringing his sister by to give me information on the baby boy my mother had that passed away not long after he was born."

"Fine."

"You really are a sourpuss these days," Kara told him as she left the room to answer the door.

"It's so nice to meet you."

"The pleasure is mine. I don't think I've ever met a detective before."

"Trust me, it's not all it's cracked up to be." Kara moved to the side so Deidre could pass her. "Hi, Aaron."

"Detective," he whispered.

"I'm sorry I had to hightail it out of your place this morning."

"No apology necessary." He reassured her placing a kiss on her cheek.

"Hello."

Both glanced toward the stairs as Kyle slowly made his way down.

Please behave yourself. Kara prayed. "Kyle, you remember Aaron, from the bar?"

"Not really."

Aaron held his hand out. "That's all right. It was a lot going on that night."

Kyle ignored Aaron's hand.

"What brings you here?"

"Aaron and his sister Deidre"—Kara pointed to the woman standing on the other side of the room—"are here to share some information with me." *I just told you this.* Kara glared at Kyle. "Can we have some privacy please?"

"Of course, I won't say a word. You won't even know I'm here."

I don't want you in the room while you're acting like a jerk.

"Fine," Kara said, cutting her eyes at Kyle, willing him to behave himself.

"We can sit in here." Kara led her guests to the den off the left of the kitchen.

"Deidre, you have the floor."

Aaron's sister had easy-going eyes and freckles sprinkled across her cocoa face, and her long black hair was pulled up into a thick bun with black-rim glasses perched on the tip of her nose. She resembled a schoolteacher more than a nurse. Either way, her friendly face was ideal for both.

"Let me say, it wasn't as easy to come by this information as it was the sonogram. It turns out that the baby didn't pass away. He was born with achondroplasia."

"What's that?" This new information was baffling to Kara.

"Achondroplasia is a genetic disorder. It affects how the baby grows."

Kara had no idea what any of this meant.

Noting the confusion in the room, Deidre continued, "Meaning that the baby's arms and legs could be severely short and he or she usually has a larger than normal head but a normal size torso."

"Oh, the poor baby. So what did my mother do with him? Place him up for adoption?"

Deidre just shook her head no. "According to her files, she took the baby home."

"I don't remember a baby coming to our house. This is all very odd." Kara was visibly confused.

"That's all we have. She never brought him back after that. There are no check-ups on file for him."

My mother is the worst liar. Where is this baby? "Thank you so much, Deidre." Kara stood indicating Aaron and Deidre should do the same. "You've been a great help. I have to sort all of this out," she said as she escorted them to the door.

"I'll be back to see you after I drop Deidre off at home, if that's okay with you."

"You better," Kara whispered as Aaron placed a soft kiss on her lips before exiting the house, closing the door behind him.

"I have nowhere else to stay, and I have to be subjected to you and Aaron while I'm here?"

"Only if you choose to be." Kara had reached her peak with Kyle's negative disposition toward Aaron. "But if I were you, I would try to make myself scarce when he's around. You will not make my guest feel unwelcome. Why didn't you shake his hand? What is with you lately? Are you jealous?"

"Me, jealous? I don't even understand the word."

"Good. Then back off." Kara smiled sweetly at him. "Glad we had this discussion. Now if you'll excuse me, I have work to do."

FORTY-THREE

IS CAPTAIN HARRIS INVOLVED? THE RALEIGH POLICE HAVE PUT *out an alert for Sophie. With a captain on the force as her father one could disappear easily without being detected.*

Kara entered her bedroom, abruptly stopping in her tracks.

"Hello, Kara."

"Sophie," Kara said back, thinking quickly for a way to handle this situation. "What brings you here?" *Kyle, where are you?*

"I see that brain of yours working. Your little housemate has already been put down. Such an easy target. What a shame; he was quite handsome."

"What have you come here for?"

"Why, Kara, sweet girl. I expected more from you. I've come to kill you, of course."

"Sophie," Kara spoke in calm tones, "your brother was an accident. I never meant for anything like that to happen. I am so sorry for your loss."

"I don't care how sorry you are. You're pathetic. You let someone else take the blame for your dirty little deed. You're a coward of the worst kind."

She is going to kill me. What can I do? Kara figured the best thing to do at that moment was to keep Sophie talking to buy herself some time.

"You're right. I was very wrong for that. That is the worst kind of coward, and I am not proud of my actions in any way, just saying I was young and dumb. It's inexcusable. I apologize, Sophie, for all the pain your family must have endured and is still enduring."

"Apologizing won't save you from your fate."

"You're right," Kara said as she quickly ducked back into the hallway before Sophie let off a shot. Racing against time, Kara ran into the bedroom locking the door behind her. Making it to her nightstand in record time, she pulled her gun out and squatted in the corner diagonal from the doors to wait.

Sophie didn't disappoint. She shot through the keyhole and entered the room. Kara shot Sophie's foot as soon as it crossed her line of vision, her gun still pointed as Sophie dropped her weapon hopping in pain. Angling her gun for Sophie's head, Kara let another clip shoot off. *Die, psycho.* Watching as Sophie's body slump to the floor, Kara felt vindicated. Ryan's killer was no more.

Moving past the still body in the doorway, Kara made her way to Kyle's room to see what Sophie had done to him. *How did she manage to kill Kyle and be sitting on my bed when I walked in?* Kara froze. *She's not alone.* Immediately dropping to the floor, Kara lay flat to the ground as she looked around from her limited vantage point knowing that her captain was somewhere in her house, *but where?*

Kara stay put until she heard what she was listening for: a floorboard squeaked to the left of her. He was cautious, listening for her as well. Kara held her breath as she waited for him to come closer to her so she could get him with one shot. The footsteps now were less cautious, moving with more vigor; comfortable and getting closer. As soon as the shiny black shoes came into focus, Kara repeated her motions displayed with Sophie; one bullet to the foot to knock him off balance. He screamed out in pain but held his gun intact as he went down on bended knee. Kara stayed in position waiting for him to stick any part of his body into her line of view again.

"Anthony, I know you're waiting for me to come to you," the captain called out. "I will report your disorderly conduct to the unit for shooting a superior."

Kara remained silent. The captain was baiting her trying to gauge her location. She wasn't falling for it. She lay still as did he, both waiting on the other to make a fatal mistake. After a few minutes of no sound, Kara crawled down the hall until she was parallel to the room her captain had shot from.

He was gone. Standing quickly, she followed the blood trail from his foot. He retreated to the kitchen. Kara groaned. *Great, now he has all types of weapons accessible to him.*

Instead of going through the kitchen door, Kara went out the front door, pressing her body along the side of her house until she could see through the window. Sure enough, her captain was propped up on a counter aiming his gun at the door, ready to shoot her upon entry. Quickly raising her gun, she smiled as the captain realized his mistake when he saw her through the window pane. One shot through the glass, through her captain's heart. He fell to the ground. Kara slid down to the ground hearing the all too familiar sound of sirens in the distance. She'd become all too accustomed to the sound in the last few days.

There are three dead bodies in my house. Just fabulous, she thought as the tears streamed down her face.

FORTY-FOUR

THE ECHO OF GUNSHOTS IN THE AIR COULD BE HEARD FOR miles. Though Kyle hadn't passed away in the line of duty, Kara had demanded a twenty-one-gun salute to honor him. He was an amazing friend, but more importantly, an exceptional man in uniform, and Kara was determined that everyone would recognize him as such.

"Dr. Jones, what are you doing here?" Kara was surprised to see Barbara at Kyle's funeral with bloodshot eyes.

"I heard about this, and it just breaks my heart to see us lose so many young men who took an oath to protect and serve."

"It is a tragedy, isn't it?" Kara embraced Barbara as she wept. "Will you be coming to the repast?"

"Oh, no, dear," Barbara stated between sniffles. "I've paid my respects now. I must run along." She waved as she retreated to the parking lot.

Returning the wave, Kara pulled the funeral program out of her purse. She hadn't glanced at it during the service. The service had been a fast one. One of Kyle's wishes was not to have a eulogy read, nor did he have family members listed. He was truly a loner.

White roses sparkled under the sunlight in all of their wonderful magnificence. *I can't catch a break.* Kara wanted her stalker gone. She'd lost two dear friends in the same week. *I wish even crazy people could take a day off.* Bypassing the roses, Kara entered her home. This was her first day back; she felt as if she were a stranger in her own space. With it being taped off as a crime scene for the past few days she'd been deemed homeless. *Thank God for Aaron.* As it stood, she had only returned home to pack clothes to take back to Aaron's, who had insisted she continue to stay with him, and she had gratefully complied.

Entering Kyle's room, she sat on the bed when it hit her like a ball of freezing snow: she would never see Kyle again. Her partner, friend, and protector was gone. *I'm so sorry, Kyle.* This was the second time in a week her past actions had come back to haunt her, and she'd lost twice. *People need to stay away from me. I'm a death magnet. Karma two, Kara zero.*

Turning to leave Kyle's room, a black journal was peeking slightly from under his bed. *How did the detectives miss this? Kyle kept a diary?*

"A diary? Come on, Kay A. I'm a guy. It's a journal." Kara chuckled. She could hear his voice chastising her. Sitting on the edge of the bed, she opened the journal to the first page.

June 5, 2009

Today Jaxson Lee Anthony must die. My father was a coward. I refuse to carry his last name or use the given name he and my mother assigned me. I loathe them both. No respect for either. My mother lacks courage. How could she stay with a man that was blatantly unfaithful to her? Love is a powerful thing, but I can't love her. I want to, but she is beneath me. Helping the world, yet unable to help her own offspring. Poor Kellie Lee. She never stood a chance. My mother dropped her like the plague. Bastard babies will do that to you. I could never respect a woman that gets rid of her child for a mistake she committed. That baby did nothing to her.

October 4, 2009

I found Kellie! My sister, I found her. We're in the same line of work. What are the odds, and she lives here in DC. I wonder if she'll see me. Maybe God is smiling on my sinning family after all.

April 1, 2011

My sister and I reconnected and work in the same department. Life is good. There's also this new woman in the department that is easy on the eyes. She's friends with Kellie. The captain is thinking of assigning her as my partner. She's hot. I wonder if she'll let me take her out. This job is definitely looking up.

April 25, 2016

Another sister? Are my feelings for her considered incestuous? Probably, how do I cut them off? Do I want to cut them off? What she doesn't know won't hurt, will it? Should I tell her who I am? She thinks our dad is this great guy and honestly believes that her mother was the only one. I feel sorry for her. She doesn't know our father isn't worth such love, but I won't ruin her fantasy. Kellie won't either.

She knows the truth about all of us, and even though she doesn't share the same father that Kara and I do, she respects my decision to keep it quiet and keep Kara happily oblivious. Her having to deal with her crazy mother is more than enough for any one person in a lifetime.

February 12, 2017

Someone is taunting her. She's in danger. I don't know how to protect her. Why is she a target? It has something to do with her father, but what? Who wants her dead?

February 20, 2017

I've talked her into moving in with me. This way I can keep an eye on her. I'm still attracted to her. I have to keep reminding myself that she's my sister. She's attracted to me too. Maybe I should tell her. There may be a slight chance she won't care.

March 14, 2017

This new guy is going to make me bash his skull in. Yeah, I ran his background, he checks out clean, but she's all in already. Why is she so trusting? This guy could be her stalker for all she knows.

April 9, 2017

My sisters are fighting. Pulling guns on each other at the job. It's Kellie's fault. She knows the history of all of us. Why she would marry Kay A.'s fiancé is beyond me. Women and their drama. Jason is a coward just like my father. Weak.

"Knock, knock, anyone home?" Kara shut the journal with a snap, placing it safely in her purse. Aaron had arrived to pick her up. *What am I to make of all this? Kyle was my brother? Misty is my sister? Dr. Jones is their mother? This is a twilight zone tragedy, I'm sure of it.*

FORTY-FIVE

"WHAT'S THE STATUS OF MISTY'S DISAPPEARANCE?"

"Still no trace of her. My wife is gone," came the grief-stricken reply.

Now she's your wife? "Jason, no news is good news. Meaning she is probably still alive somewhere."

"You think so?"

"I know so," Kara reassured him. "Have you put up flyers? I think you should do a press conference. Let's start actively trying to find Misty."

"Yeah, thanks, Kara."

"It's the least I can do."

Misty's press conference went well the next evening. Jason was the sorrowful desperate husband seeking knowledge on his wife's whereabouts. Someone had to have seen something. Since Kara's administrative leave had officially been lifted after the captain's death, she was making Misty's disappearance her number one priority. Her transfer stopped; she'd been able to go back to work, but with no captain, no Misty, and no Kyle, the environment left something to be desired. The thrill was gone for her.

~ ~ ~

Using her key, Kara entered the townhouse from the back door, making short work of disarming the alarm. She had waited until her mother left to walk her demonic dog,

Lucifer, before she entered. She had approximately forty minutes before her mother returned. Moving quickly, she attempted to open the basement door. It was locked. Kara figured any answers she wanted would be in the basement. Victoria never let anyone near the basement. It had been off-limits for as long as she could remember.

Pulling a skeleton key out of her pocket, she opened the door and began her descent down the stairs. Sliding her flashlight to the on position, Kara moved the beam of light from side to side, up and down, hoping that something of value to her would manifest.

Standing in the middle of the floor was a glass case with a wedding dress hanging inside. *What in the world?* Kara moved quickly toward the glass case, drawn to it like a moth to a flame. Sitting at the bottom of the glass was a purple and blue bouquet perfectly preserved.

Noticing an inscription at the bottom Kara bent down to read what it said: "On this day I wed my best friend. The love of my life. I love you." Kara stood up. *My mother was obsessed over my father. No wonder she can't get over him; her torch is still lit. She needs to allow herself to grieve.*

A clicking sound made Kara drop to the ground drawing her gun. *What was that?* Her mother wasn't due back for a few minutes. Moving toward the sound Kara couldn't help wishing that Kyle were here. She missed and needed her partner. She wondered if her stalker had followed her here.

The clicking sound came again. Kara reached the

corner where she heard the sound. Approaching with caution she rotated the flashlight around the area. *There's nothing here. I couldn't have imagined the noise, could I?*

The pitter-patter of feet above her announced that her mother and Lucifer had returned. *If she finds me down here, she is going to freak. How do I get out unnoticed?* After a few minutes with no plan, Kara decided she would just walk out. *I'm a grown woman now. I'm not afraid of my mother.* Marching up the basement stairs, she opened the door to find her mother standing right in front of her. Kara jumped back startled.

"Mom, why are you standing there like that?"

"Why were you in my basement? This is breaking and entering."

"I just want to talk."

"What do you want to talk about?"

"This has gone on long enough; I miss my mother."

Victoria's sigh lasted a full thirty seconds. Kara knew she was unwelcome, but her mother was going to have to deal with her unwelcome, unannounced visit this day.

"How can I help you, Kara?" Victoria's was tone frigid.

"Mom, you have to tell me what happened to the baby."

"You're still stuck on that? Why, for the love of God, won't you let that topic go? My goodness. On top of breaking and entering you are harassing me."

"Why won't you discuss it? I don't understand."

"Because I choose not to, Kara. I have that right."

"You're right, you do. But I know that baby came home with you from the hospital and is not dead like Dr. Jones told me. Why did you lie to her and tell her your baby died when you brought him home?"

"Some things you are not meant to understand."

"Mom, please talk to me."

"Would you like some lemonade?"

Lemonade? "Sure, Mom. Can you stop stalling?"

"Do you remember what today is?"

"Today?"

"Yes. Your father was murdered twenty years ago today."

May 21st. How could I forget that?

Victoria placed the ice-cold glass of lemonade in front of Kara.

"I don't know how that slipped my memory, Mom." Kara took a big gulp of lemonade. "Are you okay?"

"You know what, I can truly say that I am. I visited your dad's gravesite a few weeks ago and made my peace with the whole situation."

"Good for you, Mom. I'm glad to hear it." Kara let the topic of her brother drop for the moment. Out of respect for her father, she would pick up again tomorrow, especially since her mother was in exceptionally good spirits.

"Mother, I don't feel so good."

"I know, baby. Go ahead and shut your eyes. You'll feel better after a nap."

Kara had no option but to oblige as her eyes shut and she passed out.

FORTY-SIX

WHERE AM I? KARA WOKE TO A POUNDING HEADACHE, LYING on her back in what appeared to be a cage. Sitting up slowly to avoid increasing the pain in her cranium, she turned her head left to right to see if she could figure out her location. To her left, there was another cage, in it a severely deformed man staring at her curiously. *Luke, is that you?* To her right was Misty tied to a stake with logs beneath her. Bruised pretty badly, she was about fifteen pounds lighter than the last time Kara had seen her. Fresh white roses filled the room.

"Nice to see you awake, my dear."

"Dr. Jones?" Kara recognized the voice even though she couldn't see a face. Then the doctor stepped into Kara's line of vision.

"You were always the smart one."

"Where is my mother? You didn't hurt her, did you?"

"Now why would I do something like that? I love your mother."

"How is that possible?"

"Nothing is what it seems, sweet Kara. You see what we want you to see."

Come on, Kara, think. Barbara buried a daughter named Kellie, but Kyle's journal claims that Misty is Kellie. Kyle's journal claims that we are all related in some capacity. What am I missing? Kara willed her brain to work faster. *Kyle is Jaxson, Kellie was buried, Misty isn't Kellie . . . so who is Misty? The journal is a mix of truths and lies.*

Someone had tampered with Kyle's journal. *Misty is younger than me by two years. Misty was born after my father's death, but that doesn't matter. The journal says we're not related anyway. Unless we are. Deidre said he or she would be deformed. Twins. My mother had twins, but why give away Misty?* "I owed her," Violet's words rang in her head. *My mother gave Misty to Dr. Jones, who in turn must have grown resentful since she'd had to bury her own daughter. In her grief, she'd given the two girls the same name. But after giving Misty away for adoption, her name had been changed again.*

Kara gazed at Dr. Jones. "You are sick. What have you done to my mother?"

"I'm right here, cupcake." Her mother stepped into her line of vision.

"Mom, what is going on here? Let me out of this cage."

"I'm afraid I cannot do that. It's a full moon tonight. As an honor to your father the ceremony is about to begin."

Full moon? Ceremony? Misty at the stake . . . witchcraft. They're going to sacrifice us.

Barbara smiled gleefully at Kara. "I see you think you have it all figured out, don't you?"

"I'll scream."

"Go ahead, no one will hear you. This room is soundproof."

Luke began clicking on his cage. The sound was music to Kara's ears. She recognized the sound. The room was not sound proof as the two weirdos in front of her thought.

"Before you begin, can you please tell me what happened to Daddy? Mommy, please."

"I killed him," came Barbara's singsong voice. "Killed him, killed him."

That surprised Kara. As much of a lunatic as her mother was, she could see her studying witchcraft and killing her father because of what he put her through. But sweet and calm Dr. Jones, she'd had Kara completely fooled.

"He stepped out on the family, forgetting that I was the trained gunsmith in our family. My father's shooting lessons didn't go to waste. I shot your dad down right in front of his mistress's home. Good riddance to him."

"He had to go," Kara's mother echoed. "And so do his seeds. We can't have such evil spirits among us."

"Mother, you are brainwashed. Stop this," Kara yelled.

"It's too late, cupcake. Misty is up first. She completed the ultimate betrayal by taking her sister's fiancé and marrying him. That's your father's spirit running freely through her. She's possessed. We have to get rid of her."

Victoria lit a match as Misty's eyes grew wide. She was too weak to scream as the logs beneath her began to burn.

Use your brain, Kara. Get yourself out of this cage. Pulling a pin out of her hair, she was grateful she'd worn it in a bun today. While the two loons held hands and danced around the stake, transfixed by the fire, Kara quickly made short work of the cage lock and climbed out. Moving to Luke's cage Kara opened it for him. *What kind of a monster keeps a child caged for twenty-two years?* Luke would have to fend for himself to figure a way out. Kara had to focus on Misty and the best way to get her off the stake.

FORTY-SEVEN

AARON KNEW KARA WOULD BE ANGRY WHEN SHE DISCOVERED that he was an undercover special agent. His orders were to protect her by any means necessary. He'd followed her to her mother's house, watched her break in, and had been waiting patiently outside to give them time once her mother had returned home. That had been five hours ago. Knowing that she and her mother weren't on the best of terms he wondered what was taking her so long to come out. He was suspicious of her mother. She followed Kara everywhere. He knew Kara had no clue.

Making the decision to go in, Aaron exited his black sedan. He walked to the front door and tested the door handle; it was locked. Moving to the back of the house, he peeped through the window. Everything was eerily silent. Too silent. *Where are Kara and her mother?*

Radioing for backup, he proceeded with caution. Testing the backdoor handle, he prayed for luck. The gods were smiling; it was unlocked.

"Mother, you are brainwashed, stop this."

Aaron took his gun from his waistband, following the voice into the basement. He could hear talking behind the wall. *How do I get back there?* Using his flashlight, he flashed the light beam in the corners, at the ceiling, nothing. The glass case with the wedding dress demanded his attention. Taking a look, he noticed the bouquet at the bottom. Opening the latch to the glass case, he pulled the bouquet up to a standing position, and the wall where he'd heard the voices moved back, leading him to a staircase. Turning the flashlight off Aaron relied on his four other senses to get him down the stairs.

His backup would be here shortly, but he couldn't wait on them. Minutes could be a matter of life and death. With the smoke he was smelling, he was thinking the latter. Having reached the bottom of the staircase, he peeped around the corner, where he saw light, and there in the middle of the floor was a woman on a stake with a fire burning brightly beneath her. He saw two empty cages. *Kara, where are you?* Before he could move, a flash of something came around the corner passing him and racing up the stairs. *What was that?* He couldn't dwell on that, however, because he'd finally lain eyes on Kara. She was creeping up behind one of the older women. Not leaving anything to chance he aimed and fired at both women before they could think to duck.

As Kara crept up behind Barbara, she jumped when a shot rang out and then another causing both women to collapse to the floor. Dropping to the ground herself, she waited.

"Kara, it's me."

"Aaron?" *What is he doing here?*

"Yes, get up, come on. We don't have much time to save her."

Kara was back on her feet in seconds running to the stake.

"Back up!" Aaron commanded.

Kara complied with his order as he threw a bucket of

water on the fire and Misty. The flames ignored his effort.

"We're just going to have to get her down."

Minutes later the two had Misty lying on the floor, her feet and legs badly burned, but at least she was no longer on fire.

Kara sighed in relief as Misty's head lay in her lap and they waited for the ambulance to arrive. Luke huddled in the corner. Kara opted to leave him be until counselors could be brought in, not wanting to scare him further.

"I think I just fell in love with you."

"Well it's about time because I've been in love with you." He smiled as the two of them took in the events from their chaotic evening, thankful it had all come to an end.

Text Good2Go at 31996 to receive new release

updates via text message.

To order books, please fill out the order form below:
To order films please go to **www.good2gofilms.com**

Name:_____

Address:_____

City:_____ State:_____ Zip Code:_____

Phone:_____

Email:_____

Method of Payment: Check   VISA   MASTERCARD

Credit Card#:_____

Name as it appears on card:_____

Signature:_____

Item Name	Price	Qty	Amount
48 Hours to Die – Silk White	$14.99		
A Hustler's Dream - Ernest Morris	$14.99		
A Hustler's Dream 2 - Ernest Morris	$14.99		
Bloody Mayhem Down South	$14.99		
Business Is Business – Silk White	$14.99		
Business Is Business 2 – Silk White	$14.99		
Business Is Business 3 – Silk White	$14.99		
Childhood Sweethearts – Jacob Spears	$14.99		
Childhood Sweethearts 2 – Jacob Spears	$14.99		
Childhood Sweethearts 3 - Jacob Spears	$14.99		
Childhood Sweethearts 4 - Jacob Spears	$14.99		
Connected To The Plug – Dwan Marquis Williams	$14.99		
Connected To The Plug 2 – Dwan Marquis Williams	$14.99		
Deadly Reunion – Ernest Morris	$14.99		
Flipping Numbers – Ernest Morris	$14.99		
Flipping Numbers 2 – Ernest Morris	$14.99		
He Loves Me, He Loves You Not - Mychea	$14.99		
He Loves Me, He Loves You Not 2 - Mychea	$14.99		
He Loves Me, He Loves You Not 3 - Mychea	$14.99		
He Loves Me, He Loves You Not 4 – Mychea	$14.99		
He Loves Me, He Loves You Not 5 – Mychea	$14.99		
Lord of My Land – Jay Morrison	$14.99		
Lost and Turned Out – Ernest Morris	$14.99		
Married To Da Streets – Silk White	$14.99		
M.E.R.C. - Make Every Rep Count Health and Fitness	$14.99		
Money Make Me Cum – Ernest Morris	$14.99		
My Besties – Asia Hill	$14.99		

My Besties 2 – Asia Hill	$14.99		
My Besties 3 – Asia Hill	$14.99		
My Besties 4 – Asia Hill	$14.99		
My Boyfriend's Wife - Mychea	$14.99		
My Boyfriend's Wife 2 – Mychea	$14.99		
My Brothers Envy – J. L. Rose	$14.99		
My Brothers Envy 2 – J. L. Rose	$14.99		
Naughty Housewives – Ernest Morris	$14.99		
Naughty Housewives 2 – Ernest Morris	$14.99		
Naughty Housewives 3 – Ernest Morris	$14.99		
Naughty Housewives 4 – Ernest Morris	$14.99		
Never Be The Same – Silk White	$14.99		
Slumped – Jason Brent	$14.99		
Someone's Gonna Get It - Mychea	$14.99		
Stranded – Silk White	$14.99		
Supreme & Justice – Ernest Morris	$14.99		
Supreme & Justice 2 – Ernest Morris	$14.99		
Supreme & Justice 3 – Ernest Morris	$14.99		
Tears of a Hustler - Silk White	$14.99		
Tears of a Hustler 2 - Silk White	$14.99		
Tears of a Hustler 3 - Silk White	$14.99		
Tears of a Hustler 4- Silk White	$14.99		
Tears of a Hustler 5 – Silk White	$14.99		
Tears of a Hustler 6 – Silk White	$14.99		
The Panty Ripper - Reality Way	$14.99		
The Panty Ripper 3 – Reality Way	$14.99		
The Solution – Jay Morrison	$14.99		
The Teflon Queen – Silk White	$14.99		
The Teflon Queen 2 – Silk White	$14.99		
The Teflon Queen 3 – Silk White	$14.99		
The Teflon Queen 4 – Silk White	$14.99		
The Teflon Queen 5 – Silk White	$14.99		
The Teflon Queen 6 - Silk White	$14.99		
The Vacation – Silk White	$14.99		
Tied To A Boss - J.L. Rose	$14.99		

Tied To A Boss 2 - J.L. Rose	$14.99		
Tied To A Boss 3 - J.L. Rose	$14.99		
Tied To A Boss 4 - J.L. Rose	$14.99		
Tied To A Boss 5 - J.L. Rose	$14.99		
Time Is Money - Silk White	$14.99		
Two Mask One Heart – Jacob Spears and Trayvon Jackson	$14.99		
Two Mask One Heart 2 – Jacob Spears and Trayvon Jackson	$14.99		
Two Mask One Heart 3 – Jacob Spears and Trayvon Jackson	$14.99		
Wrong Place Wrong Time – Silk White	$14.99		
Young Goonz – Reality Way	$14.99		
Subtotal:			
Tax:			
Shipping (Free) U.S. Media Mail:			
Total:			

Make Checks Payable To:
Good2Go Publishing
7311 W Glass Lane,
Laveen, AZ 85339

CPSIA information can be obtained
at www.ICGtesting.com
Printed in the USA
LVHW01s2144181117
556827LV00002B/7/P

9 781943 686469